CW01501681

THE ALIEN PRINCE'S OMEGA

CLOSE ENCOUNTERS OF THE MATING KIND #1

LORELEI M. HART
COLBIE HART

SURRENDERED PRESS

constantly. Both of my fathers. First Father was king. Second Father was his mate and consort.

Only this morning, when we had eaten the first meal of the day, the king had called up a list of prospective mates. Having the screen hovering above us as he scrolled through the names had put me off my food, and I had pushed the meal away. My younger brother, Herix, sniggered. "I am so glad I do not have to worry about finding the perfect mate. I lie with whomever I choose and no one cares." That speech earned him a glowering look from our parents.

And now as the air crackled and the light transformed from purple to silver, I was contemplating breaking a law. I wanted to see my future. In generations past, soothsayers had terrorized the population by predicting miserable fates for those who came to them. And driven by greed, they insisted destiny could be massaged and shaped if they received large amounts of wealth.

Soothsayers lived in the shadows, their practice no longer accepted as it once was. It was a trek from the city to find the one I wanted, and I had given my bodyguard the night off, saying I was staying in the palace. I snuck away and waited until nightfall before striding away from the city, along a path lined with long, feathery grasses in multiple colors, which were dotted over our planet. Each one represented a different food group, available for anyone who was hungry.

In daylight, the fronds on the gray ones glistened with droplets, available for any traveller to quench their thirst by sipping the beads of water. At night, they curled inward, replenishing their supply for the following day.

The village I was seeking was over the other side of a river, one in which a torrent of water flowed downstream, tossing and rupturing anything that got in its way. But my people had developed a skill over millennia that allowed us to cross by harnessing our power. Being able to regulate the heat in our hands and feet, anywhere from freezing to the heat of a thousand suns, had its benefits.

I placed one foot on the surging water and it turned to ice. Another and another. I walked slowly, one foot on the ice groaning beneath me, the other in the air, waiting until I was standing on something solid before lowering the second. When I leaped onto the river bank on the other side, the river splintered the ice into shards and swallowed them as evidence of its rage.

Vines brushed over my head and whispered, "The King's son," and "What does he want here?" as I scrambled along the path leading to the village. And when I reached my destination, I stood at the entrance and waited as my eyes adjusted to the darkness. Ancient trees grew overhead, protecting the settlement from the moons.

Slivers of light peeked through the gaps in the canopy as I stalked to the hut at the end of the path. Low whispers followed me, accompanied by grunts and rustles as I passed each dwelling. But I ignored them, safe in the knowledge no one would hurt me. Despite living on the fringes of society, First Father kept us safe from our enemies, protecting the village dwellers from marauders.

Standing outside the hut, I searched for a sensor or signs I was being monitored. Our technology had developed a way for buildings and individual rooms to recognize their owners, occupants, and approved visitors, allowing them to walk through the walls by rearranging our atoms. But here I found none.

"I am honored by the presence of King Savvair's

eldest offspring." The scratchy voice at my shoulder had me planting my feet on the ground and standing rigid while a woman appeared and circled me.

"I wish to seek your guidance." *Soothsayer Idda.* I did not say it out loud, fearing word would get back to my fathers.

"Come in." Idda grabbed a knob on the wall, an opening appeared, and I walked in after her. She settled in a rickety chair and bade me sit on the floor at her feet. As a prince, I had never lowered myself to anyone but my fathers' feet, but after a moment's hesitation, I did as she asked.

"What is it you want of me?" She placed a hand on my head, and warmth radiated, not hot enough to cause pain, but it relieved my body of stress.

"My father, the king, wishes me to mate."

"Soon," she murmured, her eyes closed as her body hummed and swayed.

"Yes. But my true mate is disguised. If I do not find him and make him mine, he will be lost. And another will be chosen for me."

"He is not hidden, but he is happy. His occupation brings him great joy."

Not a prince. A worker.

"Please show him to me so I can present him to my family."

Her eyes snapped open. "He is not from Thulnara."

My head jerked backward. No wonder I could not find him. I must journey to another planet. "Tell me where. Please, my future is in your hands."

"He is on Earth, the blue planet."

"Earth!" I shouted. "The small planet in a distant galaxy which my grandfathers explored, deeming the people and their technology light years behind ours, and vowing never to make contact with Earthlings again until they were more advanced? That Earth?" I paused for breath.

She nodded.

It was not what I had been expecting. My life was about to change in ways I could not imagine.

2

HANSON

"YOUR SWEET GIRL IS PERFECTLY FINE," I reassured Astor, who'd just brought in a stray. It was his second one, the first living her best life as his inn's mascot.

"Are you sure? She's been hanging around my place, but I thought she was just a wanderer and didn't pay it much mind... well, some mind because she's so incredibly sweet, but you know." He reached down to pet her. "But she's been whining outside the window lately and the sound was different somehow and... are you sure?" And that right there was why he was both a good cat dad and a great father. He noticed little changes others might not.

"She's fine aside from no chip. Nothing about her says she has a home." And my gut said that was intentional thanks to the news I was about to give him. "But in another week or so she won't be the only new cat at your place." He tilted his head in confusion and I could see the moment it clicked.

"Oh. Babies. What do I do for her?" We spent the next half hour planning for her impending motherhood, from how to introduce her to Tiger Lily, who I was sure already liked her given that they talked to each other through the open window, down to giving her a place to feel safe giving birth and what to do when the birthing began, including calling me. By the time he left, I was confident he felt comfortable with all the knowledge and excited to go home and tell his mate about the exciting news.

I started to close up for the day. He was technically after hours, but I never had the heart to turn away a patient, especially when someone was willing to help a stray. Unfortunately, this place had their fair share of them. People would get a cat for their summer place and then just leave it. It was part of the reason most days I loved animals more than people.

How can you have a fur baby and just leave it?

Babies. My mind kept wandering back to them, and

not the ones the sweet cat was about to give birth to. No. Mine was wandering back to a babe that couldn't be and yet was as real as I was.

Every night for over a month, when I fell into a deep enough sleep to dream, I dreamed the same thing. I'd be lying on the softest bed I could even imagine, my heart filled with a contentment I'd never experienced in real life. In my arms I held a babe who suckled at my chest, happy sighs between each suck.

He was my child and I loved him so completely. Only he couldn't be mine. He wasn't human, and not like in a shifter way. I'd treated enough shifters to know their babies were not born with a blue hue. Not oxygen-deprived and dying blue, either. Closer to a neon blue with warm undertones. He very much wasn't from this world.

Not that I cared even one iota. He was absolutely perfect exactly as he was, blue and all.

I was happier there in that dream than I'd ever been in my waking hours, and I was already a happy guy with a very happy life. This was just different somehow. More... I guess was the best way to put it.

And each morning I woke up in a sort of mourning, missing him so terribly it was hard to breathe. And the kicker? I should see someone about it, get some help to break this cycle, but the longing to see him again was what got me through each day, and the thought of intentionally taking that from myself—it was too much to bear.

So just like I did every evening, I rushed through dinner and climbed into bed to see my baby. It wasn't healthy. I understood this, but it was like I was being beckoned from elsewhere and it was almost beyond my control.

I closed my eyes and counted myself to sleep.

And just like every night, I woke up with my sweet baby in my arms, only this time something was different. Something was off, tainted even.

"Who's there?" I called out, sensing a presence I never had before, one that was far from comforting, but also not dangerous.

"You are dealing well with your preparations, I see," she said in a stilted voice, as if she weren't human but also not a computer.

I couldn't see her, not her face or her hands. She was in a cloak like you'd see in old movies as they ran through the moors, the hood pulled down enough to block her face, her hands tucked in the sleeves.

"I'm tired." *What was I saying? She didn't need to know anything about me.* "I mean who are you?" *I fortified my voice.*

"My identity is of no consequence. Just know this: He will be there soon and you will once again sleep in peace."

And just like that, she was gone and I was wide awake, tears pooling on my arms as my baby was once again yanked from me.

But he was coming. The weird lady in the cloak who came into my dream said so. And that was what had happened. This dream was different, not just because of her being there. No, it was different because she was real. I knew that in my core. Whomever that woman was, she'd come to visit me and let me know my baby was coming.

And more than anything, I wanted to believe her.

3

KAGIN

I SPENT the afternoon following Soothsayer Idda's pronouncement in the palace library, researching Earthlings and their blue planet. The information had been provided by my grandparents long before First Grandfather had died. The pair of them were explorers and had headed a team of scientists and anthropologists studying known and unknown worlds.

At first, I wondered how out of date the data was, but after reading a handwritten note from Second Grandfather which said, "Little will change on Earth from generation to generation," I was reassured. And while it was helpful knowing what I was reading—

inhaling was more like it—was current, I worried how my mate would adapt.

I had not slept, not even a moment, since Idda had given me the news about my Earthling mate. As a prince and heir, I had accompanied First Father on diplomatic missions to distant planets. But none of the people we met were my fated mate. I was over-joyed that he existed and the universe had not played a cruel joke expecting me to live my life with someone chosen by others.

My parents had a love match and I wanted nothing less. The galaxy was littered with couples who had been matched by their families. And while some were mated happily, others lived separate lives, anger infecting them at being denied happiness.

My mind wandered to me introducing my mate to Thulnara and its many wonders. Was he pining for me? Had he been searching all of Earth's nooks and crannies hoping I was nearby? I had to find him and soothe his worries. Him understanding that he would be a prince and Second Father to our babies might concern him, but those worries would vanish once we mated.

But my grandparents had not taken their team to the

blue planet, so they themselves had noted minute details such as some Earthlings wore *suits* and hats and went to work carrying a *briefcase*, while others wore *overalls* and carried a *lunch pail*.

Their mates stayed home with their offspring and wore an *apron*. They enjoyed leaning over *white picket fences* chatting with their neighbors, but spent hours cooking and cleaning. They were always happy, and the little ones were bathed and ready for bed, and dinner was on the table when the First Father walked in the door.

In return, First Father would hand his mate dead plants or boxes of small brown things which reminded me of animal droppings. Ewww. And they ate them, and the children did too. So much ewww. I shuddered.

A small note at the end mentioned how valuable *television* was in informing them about life on Earth, and I learned that the opening at Idda's home was a *door*.

I puzzled over the details of one person working and the other staying home. If my mate wanted that life, I would give it to him gladly, but if he wished to continue working, we would share the children's upbringing.

Herix and I had had nursemaids and tutors from around the galaxy, some present in person, others appearing as holograms from far across the universe.

When the king stepped down and handed me the crown, my mate would be my consort. It would be a huge change from his present life, whatever that was. But that would not be until we were long mated and our offspring grown.

But as I continued my investigation, there were also stories of people on Earth who looked, spoke, and acted differently who were treated badly, and that had my hands clenching, a fierce rumbling in my chest. The desire to protect my mate, though I had never seen his face, was overwhelming. No matter his appearance, I would love him unconditionally and protect him with my life.

And that had my thoughts turning to the mating. The act of us joining our bodies, pleasuring one another first, producing children later. My member swelled as I studied an Earthling's anatomy. The Thulnarans I had lain with were always more than satisfied with my performance and I with theirs, the cries from our all-night sessions ringing through the palace until Second Father would send a message telling us to be quiet.

Earthlings were soft and fragile, and I stroked the image that hovered above me, turning it one way and the other, as I peered at the dips and planes on their bodies. Would my mate break when I entered him? I was at a loss after peering at the diagrams. An Earthling's rod was tiny compared to my own, and I studied the arrows and the numbered steps my grandparents had written.

A put his member into B. That was me, I was A. I puffed out my chest. But B lay there and waited for A to finish. And B then spurted over the bedding, himself, and maybe A. And A fell asleep, leaving B staring at the ceiling. After staring at the old sketches—why were there no photos, were Earthlings shy—I noted something odd. B's member just flopped around. Why was it not inserted into A?

Curious. But I had no time to consider it further. My mate was waiting. Idda had pinpointed his location and I had the coordinates in my pocket. I had chosen the changing of the guard for my escape. I hated the word escape because I was not a prisoner, but I should have informed First Father and been guarded by a specially chosen team.

But I had to do this alone.

There was a lot of pomp and ceremony when the guards changed shifts, and I snuck out of the library to a room under the main building. The palace had been built over a vortex which allowed us to travel anywhere in the galaxy. The sensors recognized me and I swished through the walls.

I am sorry, First Father and Second Father. I would deal with their anger when I came back with my mate. Would I be stripped of my skill, like a common criminal, to freeze or boil things with my hands? That ability was a birthright, but at a very basic level. Increasing the skill was earned, step by step, and I had achieved the highest stage.

So be it was my last thought as I entered the vortex.

4

HANSON

I NEVER FELL BACK ASLEEP that night and had slept horribly ever since, not dreaming. Or if I had dreamt, not of my baby.

He will be there soon and you will once again sleep in peace.

Those words were the only thing that kept me going. My babe would be here soon. Some person I couldn't even see the face of told me so in a dream so it was true. Just thinking about it logically had my head spinning. Instead I opted to just accept it and go on with my day.

And it was a good day too. All of my patients were there to get vaccinations or to check their healing from something previously treated, and each and every one of them was doing great. I even had someone come in with their pet turtle to see if his shell was too small, which of course wasn't a thing, but seeing his little face added a level of happiness to my work.

I began to close for the day when my phone started to ring at the front desk. I ran to it and answered, "Vet Hans—" and was cut off by a sob.

"He—I—help—" The person at the other end was distraught. That was about all I could suss out.

"Tell them corner of Willow and Maple by flea market field," someone shouted from a distance. Or maybe nearby. It was difficult to tell with the sobbing.

"Do you need a vet?" I clarified, in case they needed an ambulance.

"Yes." Another sob.

"I'll be there, but this is my land line and I'll need to hang up. If you need me, call back and it will forward."

They reassured me they would with a snotty "okay."

I gathered my emergency bag, unsure what I'd find there, and ran to my car.

The drive was short and it was pretty easy to see who needed me when I arrived. Two people stood over an animal, I couldn't tell what kind. I stopped the car and ran over to see a dog lying on their side—a dog I recognized. *Maggie.*

"Was she hit?" I knelt down.

"No. Yes. We don't know. She's just lying there." The man whose voice I recognized as the one who gave me directions spoke, the other man snuggled into his side, clearly distraught.

"Maggie dear, did you get out again without permission?" I held out my hand and she licked it. "I'm calling your papa." I gave her a pet and stood up.

"That's just Maggie. She's older and has some mobility issues and sometimes forgets and acts like a puppy, only to wear herself out to the point she can't stand," I explained and then called her owners to come get her.

It was then that I realized, for the first time since I woke up from *that* dream, that I felt fine. No, fine wasn't the word. I felt me, but better. Me in a hug? It didn't make a lot of sense, but I was going to enjoy it while it lasted.

"So she's just laying there?" the second man, who had since introduced himself as Gus, asked.

"Pretty much. Best we stay near her so she doesn't get hit, but she's fine." It wasn't the most ideal of situations, but she was a happy, happy dog, and at the end of the day that was what mattered most.

We waited until the owners arrived and loaded her in the truck with a great big thank you and an offer to pay her bill. Which was ridiculous. I hadn't done a thing and I was heading out anyway.

I walked the couple who found Maggie to their car. I didn't need to. They were adults and the dog in question was as fine as she ever was.

Dawdling. That's what I was doing. Dawdling. For some reason I wanted to be here, at the side of the road, in front of a closed flea market. And really, wanted wasn't the right word. More like belonged. I belonged here—leaving was wrong.

"See you, Doc," Gus called from his window. "We'll wait to make sure your car starts." Which was a nice, but extremely unnecessary thing for them to do.

I forced myself to walk the short distance and got inside, starting it up.

They didn't leave, flagging me ahead of them. I knew in their own way they were helping the single omega. Times had changed and omegas were no longer treated as less—weaker than... not really. Sure, some still felt we belonged in the home popping out babies, but for the most part, alphas and omegas could have and achieve the same dreams now.

Heck, I was a vet, something my grandfather longed to be, but faced too many stumbling blocks on his way there thanks to his designation. Things had really come a long way... so far from where they were only two generations ago that I often forgot they still weren't perfect until moments like this. Moments when I drove out ahead, letting them see I was fine and not in harm's way—harm from the rampant serial killers, boogie men, and aliens who were out there waiting to strike once an omega let his guard down.

Leaving hurt. Literally hurt. I felt the pull to turn right back around. I needed to be at the flea market. She said I would sleep peacefully once my babe came, but I needed to be peaceful while awake too, and I wouldn't be able to do that until I got back there. Not even a quarter of a mile down the road, the urge to go back became unbearable. I just couldn't do it... couldn't drive away.

I turned at the next crossroad and circled back around to where I began, so focused on getting back that I almost missed the man standing in the road right in front of me. I slammed on the brake and swerved the car, ending up off the road and partially in the field not far from where Maggie had been, my heart pounding in my chest, but the feeling of home and peace slamming back into me.

Maybe I died in the crash. It was the only explanation.

5

KAGIN

I HAD TRAVELLED through the vortex countless times, but never alone. First Father was usually with me, plus a team of bodyguards. Once I came of age, I had conducted diplomatic missions without either of my parents. But arriving on another planet with no guards alert for danger or them canvassing the perimeter before allowing me to follow them was a first.

Jamming my feet on a hard surface, I crouched low, wishing I had a weapon. I had no need of one at home, though my bodyguards were armed. The only one I possessed was an ancient carved piece of metal presented to me during a ceremony when I reached maturity. It had been passed down through the generations of kings, and its sharp edge could cut through stone. The weapon hung on the wall in our great room, a reminder of our past, present, and future glory.

The darkened sky and artificial light blazing from tall posts beside the road showed me it was evening. Slivers of not silvery but colorless beams had me glance upward, and I gasped. It was true. There was only one moon. My heart ached thinking of how lonely it must be. The palace library had no record of what had happened to its mate and I mourned its loss.

Loud voices, sobbing, and a vehicle pulling up caught my attention. Someone stepped out, a bag in his hand, his features clouded in darkness. Vibrations radiated over my skin and my body quivered, accompanied by a low hum. My member swelled. *It is him! My rupling.* My future was assured and I would not live out the rest of my destiny alone—unlike the Earth's moon—or worse, matched to another.

But with his face shrouded, I could not approach him.

And it was then that the solitary moon shone on

him, the weak light illuminating all of him from top to toe. Both my hearts were full and beat loudly, but he did not look my way. I straightened my pants and the tunic which reached my knees and fingered the soft fabric that kept me warm in the cold months and cool when the suns stayed long in the sky.

I took a step toward him and halted. He spoke to another, their heads close together. Rage built inside me. What if the soothsayer had made a mistake? Or she had tricked me in making me leave Thulnara? I may have endangered our family and all who lived on our planet.

But the Earthling was my destiny. Every part of me, including my member, pulsed with heat. He was the one I had been searching for. And yet he was deep in conversation with the second Earthling. If after breaking the rules and traveling a long distance, this man was not meant for me, I would crumble and my hearts might freeze.

I leaned on a wall and hunched over deep in thought, but my body jerked up, tense and alert, when my intended mate spoke, his voice sending tiny bumps prickling over my skin. *My love. I am here.*

He knelt on the hard surface and bent his head. It was then I noticed an animal lying in front of him. He was caring for the beast, talking and brushing a hand over its head. A kind and gentle Earthling. *How lucky am I?*

After adjusting my tunic, I prepared to meet him but almost forgot the glamour, the illusion that allowed me to appear much as Earthlings did, except for my skin. The glamour faded the color, but left me with a bluish tinge around the edges.

On Thulnara, I appeared as everyone else did. From the front I was humanoid, but my back was covered in scales, a remnant of our distant ancestors. On Earth, the glamour presented me as human, and I activated it from the pulse point behind my ear.

My fated mate would not need the translator. He would understand every word I said. Other Earthings would not. I was hoping to introduce myself and return with him to Thulnara before my absence was reported to my parents.

But as I strode toward him, he turned. He recognized me, my scent. I outstretched my arms, ready to welcome him, but he jumped in the vehicle and drove away. The other Earthlings peered at me before departing, and I was left alone, my arms out in front of me.

He had rejected me. A fate worse than never finding your true mate. He didn't want me. Was my smile lopsided, did the glamour not work as it was supposed to? Perhaps he had mated before I arrived. But as I stood wondering if I could follow him, a car came around the corner, its beams trained on me. As I was about to step out of its way, it swerved, making a loud screeching noise, and ran into a wide, empty space.

Him. He came back! I ran to the vehicle as he stepped out, a hand to his head.

"Kagin." His eyes ran over my clothing, and I was sure he was envious. *Do not worry, rupling. The palace tailors will outfit you in the finest tunic.*

"Sorry."

"I am Kagin."

"Oh. I'm Hanson."

Hanson. My mate has not only a face but a name. He pressed his fingers over his eyes. Was I supposed to do the same?

"You know, standing in the middle of the road at night isn't the smartest thing," he said.

I grinned at him, my heart almost thumping out of my chest.

"Do you live near here?" he asked.

"In another galaxy."

"Is that what the kids say these days? I'm an old fuddy duddy, I guess. You're on vacation, right?"

I sniffed him. "Maybe." I had learned that word from my grandparents' notes. I supposed traveling a long distance was a vacation. I was giddy he understood me. He was my one true mate.

He peered into the darkness and then put his head to the side. "Can't believe I'm saying this."

"You can, Hanson."

"Ummm... if you don't have a place to stay, you can come home with me."

"Just for a while." *Until we leave.*

6

HANSON

"JUST FOR A WHILE." The cadence of his speech was off. Not by a lot, but by enough that I suspected there was more going on here than just being almost hit. The doctor in me went straight to the beginnings of shock.

Had he been human, I'd have called for an ambulance. But he wasn't. He was some kind of shifter, of that I was sure. I just couldn't place what kind.

From a young age, I could scent shifters. If I had a dime for every time I was scolded for being rude to someone for asking them why they scented the way they did as a small child... It wasn't until I was in vet school and had a shifter roommate that I discovered exactly what I was

scenting. Being human, I wasn't able to differen-
tiate types, but I at least knew who I was in a
room with.

It wasn't just something I could mention, as some
packs were very old fashioned about what happened
to humans who discovered their kind. And by old
fashioned I meant I'd be challenged, left to bleed out
in a circle surrounded by shifters cheering on my
death. No. It was best to play dumb, while still
protecting him.

"Your vehicle is nice." He sat beside me—door open
and seat belt untouched.

"Thank you." I climbed out of the car and fixed both
for him. If he continued to be this out of it, I was
going to call one of the people I knew in town who
might have a doctor who could help him. We'd just
have to wait and see.

We drove back, neither of us speaking. And really, I
was still shaken up by almost hitting this man. But
also—it was so much more than that. I felt all these
emotions rushing into me at once. I was scared and
worried for the stranger beside me. Close to the
surface, I was furious at myself for almost running
him over. And then there were the layers of attrac-

tion and lust building inside of me so inappropriately.

I was the one who was supposed to have the clear head and take care of him, and where did my mind keep wandering? Right back to the stranger, or rather, to my cock, which was far from behaving.

"This is me." I turned into the driveway. "Let's get you inside, and maybe I can make sure you're fine?" I hesitated to ask, but something said that me asking before he made the choice to enter my home felt like a better idea.

Not that any of my ideas since I nearly ran him over could be considered exactly good.

"I assure you I have never been better." He faced me, the light catching his face at just the right angle to give his skin the bluish hue from my dream. Maybe I should be the one asking him to check me out.

"Okay." I got out of the car and waited for him to follow, but he sat there looking out the passenger side window instead.

I was about to come around to see if he needed any help, when the door clicked open and out he came.

"I apologize. I had to reverse your motions," he said. It finally started to sink in why he had been so unwilling to tell me where he was from. Now that I'd heard more of his speech, I could tell English wasn't his native language. My guess was that he technically wasn't supposed to be here.

I made a note to not ask him any more about that.

"We'll go in and I can look you over and possibly get you something to eat." I smiled in what I hoped was a welcoming manner, holding my bag in front of my too tight pants.

"You would like to share a meal with me?" His eyes lit up as he asked. Poor guy must have been so hungry.

"I would love to. Let me see what I can whip up."

I led him inside and offered him a place to sit in the kitchen and started to look around for the best thing to cook in the shortest amount of time, glad I had been too lazy the night before to make my cube steaks.

"Chicken-fried steak work for you?" My grandfather used to make it when I was little, and it had been one of my favorites ever since.

"Chickens are going to do the cooking?" For a second I thought he was serious. But of course he wasn't. Chickens can't cook.

Remembering English wasn't his first language, I explained how it was cooked and why it was called the objectively silly name.

"Sounds delicious. May I help?"

"Next time. You just relax. I did almost hit you with my car, after all." I might've said it in jest, but the guilt was still there. "Is your car there? Do you need a ride back to get it after dinner?"

"No vehicle. But maybe you can direct me to a boarding house where I might inquire about a room after we share the meal of beef pretending to be chicken?"

"I don't think you'll find a boarding house in the entire state. They no longer exist, but there are a few bed and breakfasts and inns." *But please don't go there.*

There was no reason for me to feel this way, but then again, when did feelings care about reasons?

"That would be amenable."

He was leaving after dinner. I let out a little sigh as I fished out my cast iron skillet that had once been my grandfather's. At least he wasn't leaving yet. That was something.

7

KAGIN

COOKING the dinner would have been faster if Hanson had let me help. Putting the meat in my palm would have seared it instantly, but humans did not have that ability. And this was his home, his kitchen, so I said nothing. Besides, I enjoyed watching him except when he hit the beef, which was pretending to be chicken, with a hammer. I pushed the chair back and stood up.

"Something wrong?"

"Second Father used to punish me and my brother, but never with a weapon. That meat must have been very bad."

He opened his mouth as if to reply, but instead poked out his tongue and licked his lips. I did the same. Droplets of water appeared above his mouth, and his eyes glazed over as if he was in a trance. I leaned forward, ready to capture them with my tongue, but he blinked and his body trembled.

Hanson went to the ice box.

"Wine." He held up a bottle.

I peered at the label. "Is it?"

"I mean would you like a glass?"

I nodded, unsure what I would do with it. But when he poured the liquid into two glasses, he offered one to me and I drank it all. But judging by his expression, that was not what he had expected. "So good." I wiped a droplet from my mouth, and Hanson sighed and nibbled his bottom lip.

But as my prospective mate prepared the meat, green vegetables, and potatoes along with a brown runny liquid, I changed my mind. Wine was the best thing I had ever tasted. The room appeared hazy, and I squinted at Hanson as he put the food on the plates. With a hand on my belly, I opened my mouth to speak, but a high-pitched giggle bubbled out between my lips.

He shot a glance in my direction. "Everything okay?"

More uncontrollable laughter darted out, and I slapped a hand over my mouth. "I am so happy to be here, my rupling," I explained in between plucking my bottom lip with a finger and going, "Beeb-weebbeeb."

He raised a brow. "Sounds like we should get dinner into you."

I stabbed the food, held it in the air, and snorted with laughter, my shoulders shaking, before shoveling it in my mouth. Hanson mumbled something about "meds" but I was concentrating on him placing a small piece of meat between his lips as he chewed it slowly.

I chuckled, the happiness inside simmering as I mimicked his nibbling. He muttered, "No more wine for you," but I was busy staring at his huge brown eyes.

After the meal, he led me to the vehicle, his hand clamped on my arm because I could not walk in a straight line. He strapped me into the seat and took me to a bed and breakfast. I guessed they had beds and served the meal Earthlings called breakfast. My head was still fuzzy. There were so many missing pieces of information from the palace library regarding Earth. I would have to update it when we returned home.

"This is a nice place. It's close to the beach. The owner is a friend."

"Wine makes everything different." I grinned at him, not wanting to leave his side.

"Yes. It was nice meeting you, Kagin." I put out my hand and trailed my fingers over his.

"Tomorrow," I told him, hoping I could reveal who I was and we could go home. I pointed upward, but Thulnara's galaxy was not even a speck in the sky.

"Goodbye." His voice quivered as he got in the vehicle and drove away, and I staggered inside.

A man behind the counter said something, and I clasped his hand. He was not my rupling and we could not understand each other unless I activated the translator in my palm.

"Nice to meet you." He then asked me to fill in a form, but my head was still spinning, so I pulled out a handful of money and stuffed it in his hand.

Again he opened and closed his mouth and words came out. I reached for his hand again and he tried to shake me off. "Sorry, buddy. I need a credit card. And what's with the hand-holding?" He tried to push me away. "Also, you need to see a doctor. You're kinda blue."

As I didn't have what he needed, I bowed and walked out. Hanson was right. The bed and breakfast was close to the water, and I wandered onto the sand and lay down. The warmth seeped into my back as I studied the stars, none of which were familiar.

Hanson had fed me a typical Earthling dinner. I needed to respond, but I wasn't returning to Thulnara to collect my favorite food. I closed my eyes, and when I opened them, one lonely sun was rising and warming the sand beneath me, which had grown cold.

On either side of me, long grass swayed in the breeze, and it reminded me of the ones at home, though these were all the same color. I was used to different colored grasses representing all the food groups. It would have to do, and I pulled out two clumps and headed to Hanson's by following his tantalizing scent, which still filled the air.

He came to the door. "Kagin. I was worried about you. Lennox called me saying you'd left."

"For you," and I shoved the grass at him.

"How nice." I was not an expert on Earthlings, but his voice and face did not match the word 'nice.'

"Try it." I grabbed the grass and tapped his lips with it, but he leaned away and made a strange sound.

"Like this." I chomped on a mouthful and immediately spat it out. "Ewww."

Hanson put his hands on his hips. "Are you still hungover, or is this some weird shifter crap you're pulling?"

"Shifter?"

"Yeah. Don't look at me like that with those big innocent eyes. I know about shifters."

"I can assure you," I said, "I am not a shifter."

8

HANSON

"You don't have to tell me. I know not all of you are permitted to let humans know." I waved my hand to him, encouraging him to follow me inside. "Let's get you set up with someplace to stay, and we can figure things out."

He came in and I thought back to what Lennox had said. He hadn't wanted to turn Kagin away, but something felt off about him, and he didn't want him alone either. He'd planned to call me, recognizing me from my work with his poodle, and ask advice, but Kagin hadn't given him the chance, instead apologizing and leaving.

The oddest part of the entire story? He'd held Lennox's hand. Lennox assured me it wasn't in a sexual or even too forward kind of way. He said it felt like something else—something necessary.

My guess was that not only was he shifter, but he came from one of those packs that stayed hidden from the human world.

"There is much to figure out," he agreed, and followed me in. I set the grass on the counter.

I walked back around and shut the door behind him. "Listen, Kagin. I understand you don't know me from any random human, and not going to lie, humans can be shitty. Why do you think I'm a vet? Animals are just better. But I need you to know you can trust me."

"With my life." He folded his hands into each other and brought them to his shoulder.

"I can't help you if you don't tell me the truth. I will not share your animal with others, but it might help me help you." I pressed my heel into my left eye, which was beginning to twitch the way it did when I was nervous, and I was nervous. Nervous I'd not be able to help Kagin, and he very much needed it.

"I was not deceitful when I said I am not a shifter." He sat on the couch and looked at the empty seat beside him. "Join me, rupling." There was that word again.

I walked over and sat beside him. He wouldn't hurt me. If anything, he would protect me should the need arise. I could just tell.

"What is that word you call me? Rupling?" I twisted, allowing me to look at him while we spoke.

"It is a word from where I come from. I am not a shifter as you believe, but I am not human either." He took my hand in his, but unlike the way Lennox described it, this felt personal. "I am from Thulnara, a planet a great distance from Earth, and I came here to find my future."

Did he say what I think he just said? "Why is it I believe you?" Not one ounce of me questioned his words. It was ridiculous and over the top and impossible and yet—I believed him.

"Rupling, you saw the truth from the beginning, you simply attributed it to the easiest of solutions— shifters. And now that I have taken that solution away from you, your eyes are set on the reality that is in front of you."

He flickered, a shade of blue so similar to the babe in my picture.

"Are you my son coming back from the future?" I gasped. He didn't feel like my son. No, my feelings towards him were not that at all, but I had to be sure.

"No. Why would you ask?" He leaned in a little closer. "Do you think of me as a child?"

"No. No. Not at all. It's just in the movies... nevermind." I wasn't ready to tell him about the dream. Not yet. It was a me problem and this... him here was a him problem and I needed to help him. I was just relieved I'd jumped to a very wrong conclusion. "Tell me everything?"

And so he told me about his journey and how with most people he needed to touch them to communicate and how with me... we just understood each other. I assumed it was because I was the first human he'd encountered. But as curious as I was, I refused to interrupt him. My head was flooded with all the things he explained, most of which I didn't fully understand. But I did understand the important thing; he needed help—a human who could guide him in his vague quest having to do with his future.

"I can teach you." I shored my shoulders. "I am not a teacher by trade, but in my work I do a fair bit of education."

"I already know many ways of your kind." He indicated the dead grass on the counter. "When you look favorably upon another you bring them dead plants."

I looked to the counter and then back to him and couldn't avoid the giggle building up inside of me.

"We bring flowers, Kagin. We bring flowers."

"Not grasses?" He rubbed the tip of his nose.

"No. Not grasses. Flowers. Do you accept my offer?" A growing part of me needed him to. I'd missed him in the short time he was gone, as messed up as that was. Like part of me was gone too.

"With my gratitude." He did the thing with his hands folded together and touching his shoulder, and I did the same in return, earning me a ginor-mous smile.

What I would do to get another.

9

KAGIN

"FIRST, we need to get you human clothes. A shirt and jeans. More than one pair. Maybe a nice jacket and sweater too."

Listening to Hanson's voice made my hearts beat faster, but both with a slightly different rhythm. They were singing to my rupling. I peered at my tunic and pants. "But if I remove my clothing, I will be cold when the wind blows and hot when your lonely sun is high in the sky." It had taken many years for our scientists to perfect the fabric which adjusted to the outside temperature. Removing it was only an option when we mated, and Hanson, my Hanson, was not ready for that step.

He placed a hand on my shoulder and I nudged it with my chin. "Hate to break this to you, buddy, but that's Earth for you. We bundle up when it's cold and strip off in hot weather."

Strip off? I did not need an invitation, or if I did, that was it. I tore off my tunic and stood before Hanson, my thumbs hooked into the top of my pants.

But my rupling did not react the way I had expected. His cheeks were flooded with color. First pink and then red, and he gulped as his glazed eyes roamed over my top half. He flapped a hand in front of his face while the other one clutched his chest. Maybe I was wrong, and he was ready to admit we were rupling.

Shoving his hand away, I placed my head against his heart. It was fluttering, a pitter patter, as if he was in danger and running for his life, not the melodic rhythm of my intended mate. This was bad. I grabbed his shoulders. "Hanson, can you hear me?"

He mumbled something I could not catch, and a droplet of water pooled in the corner of his mouth. Was he dying?

"Mmmm," he gurgled. "I'm... I'm fine." I pulled him close, thankful I had not killed him.

"What happened?"

"Oh. Nothing." He pulled out of my grip. "Just never seen an alien... a chest like that before." He lowered his voice. "Took my breath away. All good."

"Should I put my tunic on again?"

"Don't you dare!" he yelled. He placed a hand on my bare chest. "Sorry, I mean the world needs... I... yes, that's right... I need to gaze at it a while longer."

"I am glad it is acceptable."

"More than you know." He headed into another room. "In here, Kagin."

"Is this where I remove my pants?"

Poor Hanson, he sank onto the bed and ran a hand through his hair. His heart must have been weak. Only having one will do that. When we returned home, I would make sure he got immediate medical attention.

"Not yet." He pointed to a wall. "Open that closet, the door on the left, and you'll see clothes my brother left here. He's a fitness nut and much bigger than me. They might fit you."

I fumbled with the lever. This was not like the knob Idda had turned when she had entered her home.

"Just pull it."

I did. It came off in my hand and I gave it to him. "Now what?"

"Never mind, there's a second door." He brushed past me and my body went cold and hot. I liked it, and so did my member. My cock. First Grandfather had mentioned that word many times in his research. "I was going to donate these, but I'm glad I didn't."

"Me too." Without waiting for any further instructions, I pulled my pants off and picked up a pair of small pants in soft material with the legs cut off. "These are?"

He coughed and spluttered and gazed at the ceiling as he counted. I peered upward too and repeated the numbers along with him. "Is this a ritual?"

"Not really." His voice was high and squeaky. He must have liked the ceiling, because he studied it for a long time. "Those are briefs. Put those on first."

I followed his instructions because I wanted to do this right for Hanson. "All done."

"Now the jeans and finally the shirt."

When I finished, I tapped his shoulder. "I hope you are satisfied."

"At some point, yes. More than. I hope to be."

"Look," I told him. His expression changed many times as emotions flashed across his face. "I was not sure about the three holes. It seems as though there are one too many."

Hanson snorted, and he put a hand over his mouth. A giggle slipped out, and then laughter erupted from his lips.

"I am glad you are happy." I beamed at him.

He plucked the briefs off my head. "These are for... never mind." He tossed them away. "Though there might be chafing, but we'll deal with that later. Let's get breakfast."

I rubbed my belly. "I am ready for food."

"Great."

I followed him out of the room. "Will there be cock? My grandfather said he ate cock while he was here." *Hanson must be so proud I know English words can have more than one meaning.* I thought that was right. Or maybe it was chicken. Grandfather's notes had been jumbled on that point. No idea why.

Hanson shrieked and leaned against a wall. "At some point. I hope so."

10

HANSON

"I DON'T HAVE anything to eat, really." I'd spent five minutes staring at the contents of my fridge trying to figure out what to prepare, but all I could think about was Kagin.

Never in my existence had I ever wanted a man the way I wanted this one. But that was the thing, wasn't it. He wasn't a man. He was an alien.

Not that I was speciesist. I had thought I might be a shifter mate. I'd always felt more comfortable with them than even my own family. But then again, the shifters I knew were usually connected to my work and love of animals, so we had a bond that way.

My family? They thought I was "wasting my potential" being an animal doctor instead of a *real* doctor. Even my brother, who spent a couple of summers here before he started his family, thought I was messing up my life giving rabies vaccines and cleaning dogs' teeth when I could be in the city giving tummy tucks for big bucks. He'd always been much vainer than I and found that not only lucrative, but somehow making the world a better place.

No thanks. I loved my animals and my little tourist village.

"There are many things in your ice box." Kagin came up behind me, and it was all I could do not to lean into his chest and seek his warmth.

"Refrigerator," I corrected and shut the door. "Ice box is an old fashioned term people no longer utilize."

"Refrigerator." He ran his fingers over the brand name in the corner. "Is that what this says?"

"No. That's the name of the company that made it. And yes, there are items of food in there, but none that go together easily for a meal. Let's go out." I could take him to one of the places along the shore.

It would be fun, and with tourists in the mix he might blend in enough. Maybe.

Probably not.

"Let me get you a hat." I scurried to my closet and fished out two so he wouldn't feel alone. "Here. It will maybe make you look less... blue."

"I will not let any of my glamour down."

Glamour.

That was why his coloring wasn't always the same. Interesting. I had just as much to learn as he did, and hopefully it would take a long time and he would have to stay with me and get naked again, but this time the entire way.

"Why are you that pink tinge again with your heart beating so fast?" Kagin asked, concern on his face.

"I was just thinking of... things I should not be. Let's go eat."

"My grandfathers said that humans join hands while they walk." He held his out for mine. "They said it was a sign of companionship."

"It is a sign of courting." Gods, I sounded like an old fuddy duddy. "Dating. When two people are interested in one another as more than friends." And my face was burning once again.

"Then I doubly desire that you agree to the hand touching." Kagin watched my hand and I gave it to him, wanting it more than I should and reading far more into his word than I suspected he intended.

"Shall we walk to town or take the car?" I didn't want to let go of his hand, but it was a decent walk.

"I prefer to go this way." We went outside, our hands staying joined, and I locked the door.

"Does your dwelling face danger? Is that why you do that?"

"It's my house or home. No. I don't think so. It's a habit from when I grew up in the city," I explained. "Would you like to hear about the city on our walk?"

"Very much. I'd especially love to hear about you as a youngster." And so I told him everything I could in the time it took us to mosey to town.

I told him about my brother and I playing tricks on each other, about my favorite green bicycle that my grandfather gave me for my seventh birthday, about how sad I was to leave there when I went to college in the Midwest, and how it felt different and no longer like home when I returned to visit.

And of course, I explained all about public transportation, skyscrapers, and how different people were there than here.

"Would you like to try clamstrips?" I asked. We'd reached the junction where we were heading to pancakes or seafood. Both would do fine by my belly, but I could do either any time. Kagin couldn't. I still hadn't gathered the courage to ask him how long he was staying. I didn't want to know the answer. I wanted to live in my happy little bubble where he was going to stay and...

Whoa. The realization slammed into me. My blue baby wasn't Kagin... he was from his world, though.

What was I supposed to do with that information?

"Are they good?" he asked, snapping me to the here and now.

It took me a full thirty seconds to remember what question he was answering. "They are delicious, and if you don't like them, they come with fries, and everyone loves fries." I assumed fries were universal in the truest of senses. "And if you don't enjoy it, we can have ice cream for dinner. The shop is right next door."

"Then let's get some strips. You humans sure use that word a great deal."

Great. And now my cock was stirring and my mind was on his glorious abs.

"It's this way." If we stood there any longer, I was going to throw myself at the alien right there in the street, and that was the exact opposite of helping him blend.

11
———

KAGIN

I AM IN LOVE.

Hanson may be my rupling. No, he *was* my rupling, but fries... I had no words to describe how good they were.

"You like them, right?" he asked as I stuffed a handful in my mouth. "Would you say they're out of this world?"

If this deliciousness came from another galaxy, I had to get the recipe. "Mmmm."

"We often eat fries with ketchup." He indicated a small bowl containing a red sauce. "Go on."

I did as he asked and thrust more fries between my lips, opened my mouth wide, and shoved in the red stuff. All of it.

"Or you could dip it." He shrugged. "But never mind."

"So good," I agreed.

Hanson tapped his mouth. My grandfathers' research was detailed in some aspects, but there were huge gaps in my knowledge. Never knowing the existence of fries was a crime. I touched my mouth repeatedly too.

"You have a little something."

I put my head to the side. "I doubt there is anything about me that is little, Hanson. Which part of me are you referring to?"

Fries and ketchup flew out of his mouth onto the table, and he coughed. "After getting an eyeful this morning, I agree, and I can honestly say there is nothing about you that's small." He leaned over and wiped the corner of my mouth with a square of soft paper. He sat back. "Why are you grinning?"

I tipped my head to the side again. "I am cocking my head. Cock! So many uses for one word. I could walk around all day just saying cock and everyone would understand me."

Once again his cheeks became pink. Even the tips of his ears. "Mayo's good too." He demonstrated by putting one, just one, fry in the creamy sauce and then putting it in his mouth.

Humans ate so slowly. Why take one when you could pick up a handful? But wanting to fit in with my surroundings, I did as he had done. "Yum."

After we had finished, Hanson paid, saying, "You're my guest." Outside, we breathed in the sea and I took Hanson's hand again. I increased the temperature on my palm and the noise coming out of his mouth was like a baby animal. "I have to go to work."

"I am excited I can watch." He did something funny with his face. "Can I watch?"

"Yes, I don't see why not." He let go of my hand and grasped my shirt. "But sometimes animals are wary of strangers, so if they're afraid, I'll ask you to wait outside."

I did not understand why the creatures would be scared of me, but I agreed. When we got to the place he called his clinic, people were sitting there with their animals. The humans narrowed their eyes at me, reminding me I must tell our scientists to improve the glamour. A small hint of blue shone through even when it was on.

But the air crackled with tension as the animals—the small, smaller, and the really tiny ones—pricked up their ears, hissed, cried, and howled. Hanson giggled, but it wasn't from happiness, because the laughter never reached his eyes. He shoved me into a room and closed the door behind us.

"I do not think they liked me."

"Mmmm." He pressed something and said, "Maisy, can you send in the first patient."

A young girl walked in holding a soft, fluffy animal. "This is Annie with Thumper. He's a rabbit," Hanson explained as he put the animal on a table.

Annie furrowed her brow. "You've never seen a rabbit?"

Hanson translated for me. I shook my head. "I come from…"

"He's a long way from home," Hanson finished my sentence.

The rabbit looked at me, his long ears flat against his body, his eyes big and bulging. "I won't hurt you, little one." Annie petted Thumper and I reached out, very slowly. He didn't fidget or huddle away from me. I placed my hand on his back and warmed him. His nose twitched, and he wriggled.

"He likes you!" Annie grinned. I didn't need Hanson to tell me what she said.

"He does," Hanson agreed.

I observed my rupling examine Thumper and give him cream for his ears. After they left, a man brought his dog in who had a sore foot. And after that, a woman arrived with a cat who had an eye infection. Each time, Hanson was calm. He explained everything to the humans, and he was so gentle and kind. It brought tears to my eyes. Even the cat who hissed at me was content after Hanson quieted him.

But as animals and their humans came and went, while I admired the work Hanson was doing, it also had me rethinking my purpose of claiming him as my rupling. I had thought of it as opening his eyes to a new world, a new planet. A different way of life, at my side. Me ruling over Thulnara, us having offspring, one of whom would eventually follow in my footsteps.

His work here on Earth was important. Perhaps instead of showing him an exciting way of life, I would be tearing him away from a purpose that he loved. And by doing so, would I rip out his heart at the same time?

12

HANSON

"I NEED TO TAKE A SHOWER," I said and toed off my shoes at the doorway. It had been a great day at work, a lot of animals were helped, but with that help came the scent of anesthetics and antibiotics and such. I needed to be cleaned off.

"You can make yourself at home while I do." *Or come in with me.* No, that wouldn't be appropriate. Just because he made me feel things I hadn't felt in a long—ever, didn't mean it was a good idea to invite him into the shower with me.

"I think I take that option." He copied me, removing his shoes at the door. Damn, his ass looked good in those jeans. I put it on my imaginary list of things to buy just for him. Wearing hand-me-downs was fine, but I wanted him to feel like more than a second thought.

"Excuse me?" I asked, unsure what he meant and too distracted by his ass to process possible answers.

"I will take a shower with you."

"What?" I gasped. "You can hear my thoughts?" How much else had he heard? *Please let it not be my running commentary on his ass.*

"No. That would be helpful, though. I do not always understand what has you thinking so hard."

"But how did you…"

"You said or come in with me. I thought that was an invitation. Was it not? Is this a human custom I need to learn?" He was so serious as all I wanted to do was wish away the past thirty seconds so I wouldn't die of embarrassment.

"I spoke the words aloud by accident," I confessed.

"So is it not an invitation? Because I think I would quite enjoy it." He closed the distance between us.

"And your pants are tighter—is that not a sign you would enjoy it also?"

"I would enjoy it very much." So much that just thinking about it had me hard as a freaking rock. "But it would not be appropriate."

"Because we do not wear human rings of commitment?" he asked, referring back to a conversation we'd had on marriages.

"No. No. Not that. Because it would be taking advantage. You are in a strange place where you don't understand our ways. I would never want to take advantage of you."

"Would I be taking advantage of you?" He placed a hand flat on my chest. "Is that why your heart is beating so? I vow to you that was not my intention. I just—I enjoy your company and I find you attractive and my body reacts to yours, and I long to be more than, what did that television show say?"

"Friend-zoned?" I asked, recalling the sitcom that he'd been so entrenched in. He said that his grandfather loved our box of entertainment and he could understand why.

"That. I don't want to be friend-zoned. I feel more for you than that." He brought his hand up to my cheek. "Do you want me friend-zoned?"

"That is the last place I want you," I confessed. "I am attracted to you, but it is more than that. I can't fully understand it, but... you mean more."

"Then we should bathe together." He leaned in and brushed his lips to mine. "Humans do this differently than my kind. I like it." He did it again, and this time I deepened it, needing—wanting more from him.

"How do they do it differently?" I pressed my body against his.

"We use our tongues as well."

That was all it took to have me slamming my mouth to his and kissing him as if my life depended on it. Our lips danced together as our tongues explored each other's mouths, his hard length pressing against my own through the fabric of our clothing. "Let's shower and get my work off of us." And see his glorious body naked.

I led him by the hand to the bathroom and set the water. I removed my shirt, then my pants and my boxer briefs. He watched me, his eyes raking me up and down. I never considered my body much to look at, but the way he ogled me, I was second guessing that assessment.

"Let me help you?" I asked meekly. All of this was so new. And not because he was an alien. I had always taken the more passive omega role in my relationships. Being forward like this... it was new to me and had me thinking of other naughty things omegas never got to do. Would he like that? Would he like me in his ass? Or was it taboo like it was here on Earth for so many?

"You are thinking many thoughts." He cupped my cheeks. "What are they, rupling?" There was that word again, the one that sent a chill down my body in the best of ways.

"I was wondering—in your world, do omegas ever—do alphas like to be penetrated?"

"You are perfection." He took a tiny step closer, not that there was much room. "Please disrobe me and then bring me into your shower so I may wash your body and you may wash mine." He brought his lips to my ear. "And then if you would be so kind," his hand wrapped around my cock and I let out a hiss, "would you place this inside of me and make me come?"

Good gads. He was going to kill me, and what a way to go.

13

KAGIN

PUTTING SOAP ON OUR HANDS, we made sure our bodies were free of dirt and what he called sweat. More than once. "My cock is clean, Hanson," I panted. "You washed it two times."

"I disagree," he whispered. "It needs more of this." He stroked along one side and then the other.

"Your length is much larger than I expected."

He blinked water out of his eyes and curled his mouth into a strange shape. "All the better to fuck you with, my dear."

I bobbed my head, as his warm, wet hand gripped and pumped my cock while the fingers on his other hand slid over my backside to my hole.

"Yes, yes, please."

"Yes, what?" he asked as he lapped at water on my chest, making me dizzy.

"I want you to fill me and I will do the same to you."

His fingers slid into my hole and we both breathed heavily as he pumped in and out. "Gods, yes. Having sex once with my length inside you will be mind-blowing, but a second time with you fucking me, how will I survive?"

I could not concentrate and did not have the words to explain mating the Thulnaran way.

He turned off the water. "But the shower is tiny."

I nodded as my head bumped against the wall. "Very small."

"Unlike you." His gaze went to my cock, which was aiming at his middle. He did that very human thing of licking his lips. I copied him. "You're going to kill me doing that, you know."

I gasped and placed a hand on either side of his head. "Never."

He dragged me out, and using a piece of soft, fluffy fabric he wiped water from my body. "Get on your hands and knees, Kagin."

My body trembled as I got on the bed and a hand slid over my ass. The heavy aroma of arousal filled the room, and Hanson brought his fingers around and waggled them in front of me. They were sticky and slippery, and wanting to feel and taste every part of him, I stuck out my tongue and captured some. It was him and it was not, and I swallowed it.

"I have you in me now." Forever.

His hands spread my ass as he pushed the slick into me. There was no need, as my channel would accommodate him with stickiness, but his fingers felt so good, I wanted him to continue.

"Your member, I need it. Please put it in," I begged.

The head of his length nudged my ass, and he mumbled, "I hope I do this right. Tell me if it hurts."

My rupling. So kind. Always thinking of others. My hands wrapped about the bedding as the tip eased into me. My body quivered and Hanson's trembling voice asked, "Am I hurting you?"

"The opposite, my rupling. Take me. Push in."

Slowly he moved his cock in and my body adjusted to his size. His body stilled and I waited. And waited. Tension was bubbling inside me and my body swayed one way and the other. I wanted him to push, but he stayed so still.

Glancing over my shoulder, I peered at him. "Are you in pain?"

He shook his head as his lips trembled, and droplets of water fell from his eyes onto me. "It's... I never thought... my first time."

"Mine too," I choked out. First time with a human. My rupling.

Hanson wiped the water from his face and gripped my hips. His cock pulled out of me and he dug his nails into my flesh. Before I could count the seconds, his cock plunged into me, and we both yelled.

His voice, which had been tender, was now combined with a hardness like metal glinting under the Thulnaran suns. He thrust his cock in me, and I finally understood true pleasure and happiness.

The heat inside my body rose, and I longed to place my palms on Hanson and warm him. *Not yet, Kagin.*

Hanson slid in and out of me, and my outer body overheated and glistened with sweat. As he fucked me, I imagined the Thulnaran moons nodding their approval while my vision blurred from the water falling from my brow.

I squeezed around my rupling's member and he squealed, "Don't make me cum yet. I want to feel you and fuck you more."

There will be many more fucking sessions, my dearest one.

His hand hit my hip, and I gasped. Was he angry? He did it again, and while it stung a little, it also increased my desire for him.

"Do it again," I begged as his length slid in and out. My head, my body, and especially my two hearts were screaming, but not with pain, with lust. Hanson had captured and seized me like a warrior. He was leaving a mark on my hearts. "My cock longs to be inside you, Hanson."

"Soon, Kagin. Soon," he panted as his cock skewered me and had my body tingling.

"Yes," I cried out as I stood at the precipice. I wanted to spill my seed inside him and my cock extended, and I opened my eyes as it slid between my legs and brushed against Hanson's. He made an odd sound and then the head was at his hole, tapping against the tight entrance.

"Kagin, what's happening?" he shrieked as I surged into him. "Oh, oh, double penetration!"

Our heated bodies were fully joined. As it should be. He was so warm and tight as he gripped around my cock. One thrust from me had me mumbling, "Same time, rupling. We must finish at the same time."

"Now!" Hanson's body jerked and spurted inside me while my seed streamed into his channel.

His slurred words were, "needed condom" before my knot claimed him, and he collapsed on top of me.

14

HANSON

Nothing could have prepared me for the way it felt to have Kagin inside of me—fucking me as I was fucking him. Nothing. The scientist in me wanted to know how he managed to do that. His cock, while large, was hardly what I'd call super long—definitely not lengthy enough to do that, yet it did.

And now he was knotted in me without a condom.

I'd been so stupid. Neither one of us had any protection on, and for all I knew, we could both get pregnant. Fuck.

"Can you have babies?" I asked, his knot still inside of me. "I mean, I can't knot so maybe that's a no, but also we didn't use condoms."

No small part of me was sad about the possibility of us having a baby. Maybe it was Kagin in my dreams after all, just not *him* him, but his child. Would that be okay? I loved that baby so much, and he was but a dream.

I love Kagin too. That realization slammed into me. I loved Kagin. And not because he had just had me coming like I didn't know was possible after fulfilling a long time fantasy of mine, either. That was great and all, but it was so much more than that.

It was the way I felt when he smiled at me.

It was the little *human* things he did for me even when Kagin got them so terribly wrong they bordered on ridiculous.

It was the way he watched me as if I were the most precious thing and the most precious being in this universe.

It was the way I felt truly alive for the very first time.

"I can help create life, yes. With you? That I am unsure. Would it be, like they said on the television, a *deal breaker* if I could not give you a child?"

"I—no—I mean I was asking you if you could birth a baby the way omegas on Earth do," I clarified, and his body shook as a giggle escaped his lips. Big, strong, tough alien giggling. What a beautiful sound.

"No. It is much like it is on your planet. There is a First Father and a Second Father in the case of two men. I cannot give birth. Only you would be able to do that." His knot was slowly deflating, and I already mourned its loss. "Is that something you want? To be a father?"

His knot completely slipped out of me and we rolled onto our sides, now facing one another.

"One day I would love to be a father."

The father of my little blue baby... our little blue baby? Was I seeing Kagin's child? "Do you—do you know an old woman?" I asked the vaguest question ever. "A special old woman." Because that clarified it not at all.

"I know many. Tell me about the woman you are asking about." He pushed himself to sit and I did the same. "She is not from Earth?"

"She is... I am not sure where she is from."

His body tensed. "Earth is not a planet others are to mess with. I am breaking the rules just being here. If others are here..." His hue was changing slightly, darkening with each word. His glamour was lessening, but still holding strong.

"She was not here... not in the physical, anyways, and we will get back to the you aren't supposed to be here thing." It felt important, but not as important as the old lady. "This woman... she came to me in a dream, and there was a little blue baby in my arms, and she said *he* would be here soon. I thought she meant the baby, but now I—"

"Idda." He said the word softly and with reverence. "She is a soothsayer."

"I don't know what that means." My mind kept going to sabertooth tigers, and it sure wasn't that.

"Among other things, she knows things—things she should not. Her skill is not one permitted on my planet. I did not know she dream walked."

"Not permitted? Is she in trouble because of what I said?" Wow, I sure knew how to mess up the afterglow of a good fucking.

"If she was in difficulty for what she said to you, I would be facing similar consequences." He took my hand in his. "I sought her out. She is how I came to be on this planet."

"Explain." My stomach was starting to churn at the way his voice elevated just slightly with each word. "Explain why you are here... all of it."

"I am to take a mate, as you call it, by the anniversary of my birth. Had I not found my true mate by that time, one would be chosen for me. I went to Idda to discover where my true mate was and she sent me here... to Earth." It was so much worse than I thought.

"All those stories of people being abducted by aliens to make babies... there is some truth in them, isn't there?" It was getting harder to breathe. "You came here for a baby... a little blue baby... my little blue baby... the one in my dreams... the one I already love." I jumped off the bed. "How dare you use me like that! Is that what that rupling thing is you call me all the time? Does rupling mean baby maker?"

I ran out of the room, tears in my eyes. I loved him and he... he was on Earth with me to avoid an unwanted freaking wedding. I knew it was too good to be true. Nothing that amazing could be.

15

KAGIN

"Go away," Hanson shouted. "Just fuck the fuck off." He had locked himself in the bathroom and was resisting my attempts to apologize. "Go back to that damned fucking planet of yours and don't fucking come back."

He tossed something at the door, and I jerked backward as the sound on the other side echoed in my ear. "That is a lot of fucks," I noted. "I counted four." I leaned against the wooden panel and fell into the bathroom as the door swung open. The expression on my rupling's face was not that of the compassionate omega who tended sick animals. And it was the opposite of when we lay together, his length in me, mine buried in him.

He beat me with his fists and yelled words I could not interpret until he snapped, "I hate you," and he stalked out of the front door. "Don't follow me!"

But as I stood at the house entrance, he headed toward the beach and glanced over his shoulder more than once. On Thulnara, that indicated interest and desire. Could it be his words told me to stay away, but he meant the opposite? It was confusing, and I did not wish to make him more angry or scare him.

So, I followed him at a safe distance, but at the last minute remembered to put on the clean shirt and pants Hanson had put out for me earlier. Humans would not appreciate me walking naked on the street. And besides, after seeing my cock, they might feel bad that theirs was so small. Getting dressed was the right thing to do.

When he swung around and glared at me, I inspected flowers hanging from a basket swaying in the breeze. "So pretty."

The next time Hanson looked back, I hid behind a bush, and he yelled, "I can see you," to which I replied, "I can not see you." When he reached the beach, he took off his shoes and walked to the water's edge. I lay on my belly on the soft sand, surrounded by tall grass, close to where I had slept that first night.

"You're ridiculous, do you know that?" I poked my head up. "You can't fool me."

"I would never."

He placed his hands on his hips and scowled at me. "Get down here and explain everything. Don't leave anything out."

"Or there will be more fucks?"

His shoulders shook and he clamped his teeth over his lower lip. "Stop that." He kicked water on my clean pants. "No more fucks, no matter how mind-blowing. Now talk."

"I came here for you."

Hanson's body tensed. "To steal me away, impregnate me, and use me as a baby maker. Is your planet in its death throes? Are there not enough omegas, or whatever you call them, to populate your home?"

"Zialt."

"Huh?"

"That is what you would be called on Thulnara," I explained. "I am an izleen and you are zialt."

"Fuck that. You're not abducting me."

"And we are back to the fucks." I lowered my voice. "You said there would not be any more."

"Grrrr," he growled at me. "Oh, so your mate has been chosen for you and you threw a tantrum and decided to stick it to your dad and find a mate on Earth instead?"

So many words. "Stick it? I recall sticking..."

He held a hand against my mouth. "Do not mention cocks, fucks, or sticks. Okay?"

"You have my word." I paused. "Just not those words."

"Please explain everything slowly."

"I have never met the intended mate. I do not know if First Father and Second Father have chosen anyone, and I do not want to meet them."

"Oh." He stared out at the ocean. "I'm not second best? Your second choice, I mean?"

"You are number one." I thumped my chest. "My only one."

He grinned and then giggled. "I want to stay mad at you, but I can't."

"You would be my rupling even if you were foolish."

"Mad and foolish... forget it. That's good to know." He put his hand in mine. "Walk with me."

"I did not explain you were my fated mate because I thought it might scare you. I tried to court you as humans do."

"That was kind of you. If you'd charged up that first night, flung me over your shoulder, and taken me back to Thulnara, I could have been kinda annoyed."

"But if I'd taken you by the hand and pulled you into the vortex, that would have been all right?" He studied my face, his eyes narrowed. "It was a joke," I said. "I was trying to be funny. Humans like that."

"Sometimes." He patted my chest. "Do me a favor. No jokes." He waved to a boy with a dog playing in the water. The youngster shaded his eyes and stared at me while the animal yapped. "It's a lot to think about. Finding true love with someone from another galaxy." He stared at the sky.

"The cosmos is huge and the universe chose you. And from the moment I laid eyes on you, I knew you were the one."

He pecked me on the lips. "More please," I told him as I wrapped my arms around his middle.

"You know how I said no more fucks?" he asked.

"Yes."

"Perhaps we could reconsider," he suggested.

"I would like that," I agreed. "But first." I stopped and grimaced. "I have guessed the meaning of chafing, and it hurts."

He burst out laughing. "Let's get you home."

"One more thing I should tell you. I am a prince."

16

HANSON

I WASN'T EVEN sure why I freaked out on Kagin the way I did. Fear, I guess. Fear he didn't love me the way I loved him. Fear he'd want me to give up everything I'd worked so hard for to go across the galaxy and be the only human there. Fear that he'd leave as quickly as he came.

And now—he was a prince. A freaking prince. I'd have to really process that later. For now my brain had a thousand other things fluttering through it.

Not once did I truly believe deep down that he was using me. That was the fear talking and I needed to make it up to him. Not because he wanted or needed me to, but because I wanted to. We both had been less than forthcoming, and given the situation, I doubted either of us would've done anything different if given the chance to do it over again. We weren't ready to be that open then.

But we were now. And that was what mattered. Were there more things to say and decide? Absolutely, but we were on a good path.

"I'm planning a surprise for you." I plopped down on his lap. He was watching children's television to help pick up more English. As much as I'd love to be with him all of the time and touching him so he understood what people were saying around him, he needed this. Being dependent on me for communication was less than ideal.

"Allowing me to hold you is a surprise I quite enjoy." He wrapped his arms around me. "Thank you for accepting me, faults and all." He kissed my head, and I burrowed into him, almost forgetting I had a mission to accomplish.

"That is not the surprise. I'm going to town to gather some things to give you a human date night in." I pulled my lip in with my teeth, excited to see his reaction.

"Liquid in a bottle and corn in a bowl?" he asked, his eyes wide. "And frozen confection in the carton?"

"All of that and more." I kissed him far too briefly for my liking. "We will have lots of fun."

"I always enjoy my time with you, my rupling." He nibbled on my chin. "You want me to remain here?"

"Yes. Otherwise it's not a surprise." I climbed off his lap, adjusting my jeans, which were now too tight. "I will go as quickly as I can and don't ruin your appetite, I am bringing back pizza." I was very not good with surprises.

"You would bring me such a delicacy?"

"I would do anything for you." And the truth of those words hit me deep. I would. He was mine and I was his. There was still so much to work through and learn, but at the end of the day, that was all that mattered.

I'd heard shifters talk of their true mates and how they never once second guessed that fate brought them together, and I finally understood what they meant. I felt that for Kagin, my rupling.

"As I for you, my rupling."

I went outside and contemplated taking the car. It would be easier to carry things, but a pain to find parking. I opted to walk, the day being nice enough that the mass quantities of tourists would most likely be flooding the area.

I only made it past my neighbor's home when a weird feeling came over me. Like I was being watched but more intense. Had I just watched a horror movie I'd have argued the feeling away as me being paranoid, but I hadn't been.

I was being watched.

A few more steps and I scented Kagin, but not. Now that I knew the difference, I was confident it wasn't a shifter. Which meant one thing... another alien.

An alien watching me.

"Crap. I forgot my wallet," I said out loud and turned back to the house. The last thing they needed to figure out was that I sensed their presence. And maybe it was nothing, just someone checking up on Kagin. But it could also be someone coming to do him harm, and that wasn't something I'd allow.

The one thing that hadn't crossed my mind was that they were there for me, not until they grabbed me by the wrist as I reached my driveway.

"You," he seethed, his glamour firmly in place. He looked every bit human but off—like a computer-generated person in a movie, almost. "You do not belong to the Prince."

I tried to take my arm back so I could run. He held on tighter.

"Ow, you brute." I pushed at him with both hands. "Let go of me."

"You scent of the royal family." His spit reached my face. "He thinks of you as the lesser being you are, I see."

"Who are you?" I asked, my voice shaking.

"I am Umon, future rupling to Prince Kagin."

My stomach revolted and I almost vomited its contents right there.

"No." I refused to believe it.

The front door swung open, and out came Kagin.

"No marking, I see," the alien said.

"Do you want to be seen?" Kagin's voice was firm. "State your purpose."

Dragging me along, he walked to the front steps. "My First Father offered me to your First Father for consideration, but your First Father declined. It took me traveling across the galaxy to find you, and then to see you screwing the lesser being. How beneath you. You put all Thulnarans to shame."

"Let. Go. Of. My. Rupling." Kagin's glamour was flickering. That was not good. None of this was good.

"Rupling? Ha." He pushed me to Kagin. "Show me his mark—the one that shows you find him worthy. You cannot because he is not."

17

KAGIN

I REMOVED Hanson from Umon's grip and pulled the unwelcome visitor inside, while putting an arm around my rupling. "Do not worry. This is a problem for me to solve."

Instead of Hanson's cheeks being the glorious pink they became when he pictured us lying together, they were white. No color at all. His eyes held fear, and his hands trembled. We walked in and I closed the door before standing between my rupling and Umon. Though the Thulnaran being here was not part of my plan, I was First Father's son, and a prince, heir to the kingdom. Umon would listen to reason.

But he had traveled across the universe to find me. He was determined like the dog with a bone I had witnessed in the garden next door to Hanson's.

"Sit, Hanson." Umon opened his mouth to speak, and I shook my head. "You will talk when I give you permission." I snapped at him and turned to my rupling. "What you are about to see may surprise you, but I assure you there is nothing to worry about."

"Well, if I wasn't scared before, I am now. Thanks, Kagin." Once again, his words did not match his lips, which were set in a tight line, and his hunched shoulders.

"That!" Umon scoffed. "That is your chosen rupling. That weak, puny creature with the garbled language."

"What's he saying?" Hanson demanded.

"I must hold the Earthling's hand to understand his words," Umon spat out.

This was not going as I expected. Umon was not showing me respect, and Hanson was being the feisty human I knew him to be. "Remove your glamour, Umon," I said over my shoulder.

"In front of the human?"

"Do it. As your prince, I command you." He glanced at Hanson, who glared at him. My rupling was not weak, but the opposite. Umon and I reached for the pulse points behind our ears and turned off the glamour. Hanson let out a deep shuddering breath as his eyes were glued on me.

Not wanting to hide from Hanson, I removed my shirt. No longer with just a hint of color, my body was a deep blue. But I was facing my rupling and from the front, I was humanoid. He needed to see the real me. I had hoped this would happen on Thulnara when I presented him to my parents.

"Wait until he sees the back," Umon snarled.

"Do not move," I commanded him as I swiveled around and allowed Hanson to gaze on my body. The back of me was covered in scales, interspersed with tiny spikes. And the color on each Thulnaran was a unique pattern of green and blue streaks.

Umon sneered at me. "He cannot talk. He is so repulsed by your ugliness."

A Thulnaran would never speak to me in that manner at home. But my thoughts were all of Hanson. Afraid to face him, I studied a small tear in the couch and a container of dead plants. Flowers.

A hand, a human hand, with no power to boil or freeze, glided over my scales. "You're beautiful, Kagin," he choked out, and I swung around and held both his hands.

"As are you."

"Probably should have removed the pants." It was only then I discovered my jeans were torn, my Thulnaran form being larger than my human one.

"We are wasting time," Umon said.

Time to be the leader I was born to be. "Enough," I yelled, and the container with the flowers jiggled. He bowed his head and brought both hands to his right shoulder as I examined the shredded human clothing clinging to his body. "You are not from First Father's court, but I have seen you before."

"I am a trader, Your Highness. I travel the galaxies buying and selling goods." His tone had softened, for which I was pleased.

But I hadn't counted on my rupling interrupting.

"Come here," Hanson beckoned Umon.

"Go," I told the trader as he looked at me, confusion in his eyes.

Hanson gripped his fingers, and for the first time, Umon looked uncomfortable. "Go ahead," my rupling said as he waved his other hand. "It's all good."

Except it wasn't.

"Your First Father made a gracious offer." I touched my clasped hands to my right shoulder. "But the king did not accept. That should have ended the matter and helped you save face. But now you have stained your family's reputation."

"And yet I was right to follow you. This foolhardy venture to Earth has been nothing but a voyage to lie with as many humans as possible before you are mated."

"Kneel," I yelled at Umon, the anger which I had kept in check now bubbling out of me. Hanson's face betrayed little emotion, though his free hand fiddled with his hair.

"Permission to speak, Your Highness," Umon whispered, his knees planted on the floor.

"You may."

"You are the heir of your First Father, King of Thulnara, but if this... this human is your destiny, why have you not marked him? If he is your rupling as you say, you would have claimed him the moment you met him."

I wanted to.

Umon took a breath. "You have used your privilege to escape your true destiny—me—and come to Earth." Hanson reached out and gripped my hand, and I squeezed it. "Therefore, I have no choice but to report you to the king."

"So be it."

18

HANSON

"I DON'T UNDERSTAND." I collapsed onto the couch, my body unable to bear my weight, the adrenalin of Umon's visit too much. "Any of this."

"He is gone. He will, as you humans say, *tattletale* to my First Father about me. My father will not care where I am, only that I am with my rupling." No part of him looked nervous about that. But then again, it was his father. Why would he be?

I was the one who had the rights to all the nerves building inside of me. "Not that." My head fell back and I closed my eyes. "I mean I needed to know part of that, but that's not what I don't understand."

"Might I join you?" he asked, and I crooked my finger. He didn't sit, and my eyes opened to see him just standing there. "I will do you no harm."

I'd signalled him in a human way and he thought I was ignoring him or worse, denying him. Was that how all of this mess was? Had I missed things this entire time simply because I was human and didn't understand things he was telling me? "Please join me."

He sat beside me and I snuggled into him. "I should be mad at you or at the very least sad, but I don't know... I need this right now."

His arms came around me, giving me the comfort I sought.

"You really are stunning." I hadn't thought about that—it hadn't mattered what his true form was, at least not enough for me to even consider it. But that had to have weighed heavily on him, hiding his looks from the humans and by default me as well. "I'm glad I saw you today... really saw you."

"As am I." He intertwined his fingers with my own. "My people—when we meet our true mate, we just mark them. There is no wooing as is the way of your kind. True mates... we recognize each other and our nature takes over."

I rotated my body enough to see his face without losing his embrace. "And yet you didn't mark me?" He hadn't, my real question much more needy than that. *Am I really your true mate? Are you sure? Am I good enough, being the weak human that I am?*

"I wanted to mark you from the second I sensed you. But you are human and—"

"And not of your world and weak. I understand." That my heart was breaking.

"No. No, nothing like that." He guided me up onto his lap. "It's because if my true mate was my kind, we would both know exactly what was happening and we would be making the choice. But you—you didn't know, and if I marked you then or when we joined... you would not be making the choice, I would be making it for you."

I remembered how pissed I'd been after we made love, and that was without the marking. I'd allowed myself to get all twisted around because I was so afraid of my emotions. Had he marked me... "You're right. It would not have ended well. But now? I want you to. Mark me as yours, Kagin."

"What do you know of marking?"

I climbed off his lap and climbed back on, my knees on either side of his hips. "This is better," I said, meaning my seat. I cupped his cheeks with my hands. "I know the mating of shifters, where they mark each other with teeth and claws. Is that what you would do? Would you *bite* me?" I nibbled on his bottom lip.

"No." He swallowed. "I hate to say this, but I need you to get off my lap for a minute."

I kissed him and climbed off. If he hadn't sensed the importance of what was coming next, getting off of him would've been much more difficult. Being with him, touching him, feeling his breath—that was home.

He took my hand and led me to the refrigerator. "What I am going to show you is not meant to scare you." He took out the milk and a dish and set it on the counter.

He placed his hand on the milk carton, then pulled it away. "This is plastic." I wasn't sure if he was talking to me or himself. Kagin reached for a pot in the cupboard and poured some milk into it. "It would have—you'll see." He placed the pan on the palm of his hand and the milk inside began to steam and then boil.

"You will explain how that works later?"

"Absolutely, my rupling." He set it on the stove. "But there is more." He placed his hands on the hot pan and before I could figure out what he was doing, the milk had formed a huge ice cube.

"And you are showing me this because it has to do with marking me?"

"Yes. Izleen and Zialt are the moons of my people. They are mated, which is why we are izleen and zialt —alpha and omega." He took my hand and placed it on his shoulder and then placed his hand on mine. "To mark, we call forth the moon after our hearts, in my case, Izleen, and our hand imprints upon you."

"You burn me?" I asked. "Or do you freeze me?"

"The moons decide, but in either case it is a burn, but your mate doesn't feel the pain, not if they are a true mate. Or so I have been told."

"But I won't be able to mark you." A sadness started to bubble deep inside of me. "Maybe I could mark you in the ways of the shifters?" I offered.

"Or we can trust the moons to know what they are doing."

"You would not feel incomplete?" I could never live with myself if I was but half a mate to him.

"I already am complete, just by having you in my life."

"Mark me, Kagin. Make me yours."

"I will mark you, but make no mistake, rupling, you have always been mine."

19

KAGIN

"UNLESS YOU DISAGREE, let us mate on the bed. It will be easier and more pleasurable for you. Mating in the traditional Thulnaran way of standing and squatting would be painful for a human. Once, I..."

Hanson placed a hand over my mouth and stopped my words. "Sweetheart, when you're about to mate, you don't mention past lovers." I hardly heard the rest of his sentence, my mind concentrating on the word 'sweetheart'. A human expression of endearment.

He led me by the hand to his bedroom. "If a Thulnaran can mate standing up, so can I."

There was another matter to consider. "Would you like us to fuck the way Earthlings do?" He shrugged off his shirt and lowered his jeans, and I growled.

"What is it? Did I do something wrong?" he asked.

"You are wearing briefs and I wish to see your cock."

"Chafing, remember? That's why I wear them." He took my hand and placed it over his bulge.

My breath quickened, and I rubbed my palm over his rock-hard member covered in soft fabric. Hanson whimpered while reaching up and winding his fingers through my hair. He tugged hard, and I moaned.

"Those pants are hanging on your hips by a thread. Glancing down, it struck me I was not in human form. I was me. My rupling was looking at the real me. The blue of me, along with the scales and spikes on my back. He yanked my pants and they fell away as the air filled with the tiny fibers.

Hanson fell to his knees and stroked his fingertips over my chafed thighs. "We'll..." He kissed my blue flesh, and I gasped, running my fingers over his scalp. "Make this better." Another kiss and my legs quivered. "Later." My head fell back as his soft lips soothed my discomfort and started a fire in my belly.

I picked him up. He wrapped his legs around my waist and ground his stiff cock, still clad in the underwear, against me. The sensations in my body, coupled with the thoughts swirling in my head, had my body swaying as I placed my lips on his. He made noises like a baby cat when I sucked his lip and licked around his mouth.

He pulled back, shock etched on his face as his wide eyes searched mine and his mouth gaped. "Your tongue, Kagin. Oh my Gods. It's freaking amazing. Next time you have to suck my cock."

"I can do it now, my rupling," I panted as I slipped one hand into his briefs and squeezed his ass. I hefted him up higher and fingered his hole, so slippery and warm, just waiting for me. He moaned and opened his mouth wide, welcoming my tongue inside, as I pushed my fingers in and out of his hole.

His breathing became shallow and then sped up while our tongues battled. His hands clamped on my scales as he bucked his hips against my belly. He would come soon, and that could not happen. "No, my dearest Hanson, when we mate, I must be inside you."

"And me in you." He had finally answered my question.

He slid off my body and I removed his briefs and tossed them on the floor. I faced away from him and spread my legs, crouching a little as I was much taller. His length brushed over my ass as he squatted beneath me. Like last time, he fingered me using his slick, though there was no need. I hoped his legs were strong enough as the head of his length brushed around my hole.

Hanson grunted, probably because of the awkward position. All Thulnarans were of similar height, not much shorter as my rupling was. "My legs will take the strain," I mumbled. My thighs complained as I lowered myself onto his cock and we both groaned. "Oh, rupling. Your length was made for my hole."

"You're so slick, babe," he moaned as I lifted myself up, and with his hands on my hips, I fell onto his cock. The aroma of slick tickled my nose, making my length bob up and down.

One of his hands moved from my hip and grazed over my lower back, stroking the scales and gripping the spikes. Maybe it was my imagination, but his palm was cool, almost as if...

"Kagin." His voice interrupted my thoughts. "I need your cock in me," he bellowed. "Please hurry. I want to watch your length as it glides toward my hole." His uneven breathing told me he was quickly becoming exhausted or he was reaching his peak.

My member protruded from my body and slipped through Hanson's legs. The tip tickled his balls, and he squealed. "Again, Kagin." He gripped my spikes, using them to relieve the strain on his knees. What a clever rupling. My length circled his balls, squeezing and releasing them, drawing out a scream from him. And it probed his entrance, slick covering the head, as it nuzzled against the slippery flesh.

But Hanson, my rupling, did something unexpected. After removing a hand from my back, he grabbed my cock and thrust the head inside him, while fucking me. "You are a superhero," I panted, like the character I had seen on the television. "A super fucking hero," I added as I slid into his tight, warm channel.

"Better believe it," he squeaked as he squeezed around my length. Each time he rose up, his cock filled me, and when he lowered his body, my member penetrated him. We were mating as Thularans where the zialt controls the speed and the angle, taking the lead.

The familiar flames in my belly had sweat covering my body. My head was full of wooly clouds which sent a warning that I had to mark my rupling as we came. Flinging my arms behind me, I grasped his back and begged the universe to make it painless for Hanson. If I hurt him, I would never forgive myself.

A rumble deep within me signaled it was time, and I clamped my eyes shut and pictured my palms marking him. "Now, Hanson."

"Kagin," he yelled as he hung onto my spikes and his cock claimed my ass while my member dove into him. As he came and my seed spurted in his channel, a sickly sweet smell overlaid the scent of mating. *My hands are heating his flesh.*

"Hanson, are you all right?" I yelled, twisting my head. He was gripping me with a fierceness I had not seen except in pictures of warriors, but my mind flashed to an iciness flooding my body. Not overwhelming me, but causing my scales to crackle. His body went limp and his member slid out of me as my knot expanded and filled him to the brim. But his breathing never wavered.

Later, I carried him to the bed and he mumbled, "My rupling." I examined him and discovered the faint mark of my palms on his skin. Looking in the mirror, there was an imprint on my scales, an outline of fingers in a lighter blue than the rest. Hanson was human. How could he have marked me?

20

HANSON

"THAT WAS... wow... nothing like what I expected." I held onto Kagin as we entered his world. In my mind, I had spaceships and teleportation devices as the mode of transport, and this was... wow. "It was so fast. Like if we wanted to we could go back and forth and not be... home doesn't... never mind."

It had been two weeks since we'd marked one another, two weeks since we'd decided that nothing, not even being from different planets, could keep us apart. Two weeks since I became the happiest I'd ever been. But it was time to rejoin reality, the one that said it wasn't just us we needed to think about. Kagin had an entire planet and a family to get back to.

Aside from not wanting to avoid the inevitable any longer and needing to meet my father-in-law, we'd traveled back to Thulnara for a variety of reasons, from making sure things with Umon had just been what they appeared to be, to figuring out how it was I'd marked Kagin's back.

I still puffed out with pride each time I saw the mark. I did that. I marked my mate. He was mine.

After all this time, I finally understood the big deal. I always listened with enthusiastic nods and squeals when a friend showed their marking. That's what you do. But it had always been that—being a good friend. Now I got it. I wanted to show everyone.

"Yes, my rupling, we can go back and forth." He squeezed my hand and held it. "Our first trip will be to see First Father." It saddened me that I wouldn't meet his Second Father at the same time, but seeing I was an alien on their planet, it made sense that the king should approve of my presence first.

Me. I was the alien. That was a lot to take in, but then again, all of this was.

Not that I wasn't terrified to meet the king of an entire freaking planet.

"He will approve?" my voice squeaked. *Please let me remember all of the greetings, such as the arms being pressed together and the signs of respect.* I only had one chance to make a first impression... wasn't that how the saying went?

The walk to meet my father-in-law distracted me from my worries. The vortex was beneath the palace, but as I discovered, there were no doors. Kagin walked through walls, but even though I was on Thulnara, I was still human. My rupling had to burn holes in the walls for me.

Eventually we walked into what I soon discovered was the King's private chambers. Kagin held my hand, not only for comfort, but so that I might understand the words spoken around me.

"Son, you have been wandering the stars, I see." There was no anger in his eyes, but his posture and intonation had me unsure of where he stood on all of this. His eyes flicked to the Hanson-sized hole in his wall. "And destroying the palace."

"You see or Umon informed you?" Kagin, on the other hand, I had a feel for. Kagin was teasing. What a relief.

"His hearts no longer break for you... his gift of finding you has given him what he longed for... respect from me and the council of elders." The king took a step closer and lowered his voice, "He is quite the tracker and meant neither of you harm... he is simply Umon."

"This is my rupling, First Father. His name is Hanson and he bears my mark and I his." I moved my clothing to give him a better view.

"He is of our kind?" his father asked as his gaze flicked to his destroyed wall. I'd been wondering that myself. Could I possibly come from a line of humans who had met and mated with someone from Thulnara?

"We do not know. Does it matter?" Kagin asked. "He is mine and I am his. We are ruplings. Everything else is noise."

My stomach decided to pick then to revolt. I bent over, my hands on my middle, trying to figure out the quickest route to somewhere, anywhere not where I was about to puke. My father-in-law was speaking to me or maybe Kagin. I didn't even know. I understood none of his words.

"Hanson." A vessel was placed in front of me. "For your projectile."

I wanted to tell him I didn't need it, that I was fine. But I very much did need it and hated that puking was going to be my first impression. I barely set it down and I was whisked away to their healer, both Kagin and my father-in-law never leaving my side.

"I'm fine," I kept saying, and I was too. Just vomiting made me feel a thousand times better. "I'm just not used to such long distance traveling."

I reached for Kagin's hand, hating that I couldn't decipher what the doctor was saying, and was relieved when I felt his hand on my own.

"The mark is the sign of a true mate. This zialt is not of our kind, but he is the one meant for you out of all the beings in the galaxy," the doctor or healer, I wasn't sure the difference, said. He mentioned both in the chaos.

"Was it the traveling that made me ill?" I'd hate to be sick every time we went back and forth, but I also couldn't imagine not being on Earth at least part of the time. I would, of course, if that was the only way to keep Kagin, but I very much didn't want to.

"Oh, you are not ill. You are with child." *With child.* I was having a baby. No, not just any baby. My blue baby, the one I had loved for so long.

My eyes were blurry, already filled with tears from the joy of it.

"Rupling, are you hurt?" Kagin asked,

"Oh no, my love. I'm not hurt. I'm so very happy." He kissed me, not even caring who saw, nor did I. We were having a baby. Our sweet little babe.

"As am I." He brushed his lips on my forehead and then looked at the healer and asked, "How much time to prepare?"

"Oh you have time. The gestation is quite new."

"So we have three?" Kagin asked. What was he saying? Surely he couldn't mean...

"No. But a solid two and a half," the doctor replied, and my mind raced to elephants. I had always felt bad about them for being pregnant so long, and from the sounds of things, I was going to be pregnant even longer.

How was I going to explain that to my clients and friends? "I'm just over due by a year. No worries." For the first time in my life, I wished I were an elephant.

"I'm going to be pregnant for two and a half years?" I gasped.

"Oh, sweet rupling. Of course not. Two and a half weeks."

"Two and a half weeks?" I pushed myself up. "We need to go home. I have so many things to prepare." Even a rabbit had a full month to get ready. "I don't even have a crib." I jumped off the bed. "Come on. We have to go."

I didn't even know what my father-in-law was saying to the healer and my mate, but he was completely amused. I didn't have time to be bothered by it. I was having a baby in two flipping weeks. Two!

21

KAGIN

"WE MUST GO HOME." Hanson grabbed my shoulder, his eyes glazed and unfocused. "I have to prepare for the baby's arrival. And find a permanent replacement while I take paternity leave. And tell my friends. And and and..." He tugged at his hair as he paced my quarters.

My head swung one way and then in the other direction, making me dizzy, as I followed his progress. "Hanson," I said and reached to him, but he took no notice.

My rupling chewed his nails and held up his phone and muttered, "Not even one bar," forgetting Earth's primitive technology was useless on Thulnara.

"You should eat and perhaps rest."

"No time for that," he muttered as he stabbed at his phone and made endless lists. "Cloth or disposable diapers?"

"Babies are born all the time on Thulnara, and you took a month's vacation from your job. Your animals and their owners are being looked after by Dr. Batson."

"Mmmm."

He had gotten over his initial sickness but was wary of Thulnaran food. And while my grandparents' original research from decades earlier described some of the food they ate on Earth, I was able to update the information on the computer. When the sensor buzzed and I gave the okay to enter, the palace servant walked through the wall bearing a tray of Earth goodies.

But even that had my rupling clutching his heart. "That still freaks me out, even when I do it." Rather than rearranging Hanson's atoms permanently, our scientists had given him a temporary fix with an injection. It would last until after our little one was born.

"Look dearest, fries, burritos, salad with the goat cheese you love, and all kinds of sauces, including ketchup. And there are chicken wings too." I hoped he was proud of me not calling them cock wings, as I recalled a confusing conversion after I used the term and he thought I had said cock rings. I still was not certain what a cock ring was and this was not the time to ask about it.

"I don't have time to eat." He grimaced, but I took the tray, and once the servant had left, I held it under his nose. And he paused his frantic pacing, and a blissful expression replaced the agitated one of pinched lips and furrowed brow. "Oh..." He leaned against me as he inhaled the aroma. "That does smell good."

He stuffed a handful of fries in his mouth, just as I had done the first time I had eaten them, and picked up a chicken wing. "I'm impressed. Almost as good as the ones on Earth."

When he finished, he licked his fingers, which was an Earthling habit I hoped our baby would not develop, and I steered him to the automatic sanitizer.

"I have an idea."

"What's that?" he asked.

"I wish to show you what I did the evening I went to see Idda before she told me about you." Once outside, we followed the now familiar path and paused at the place where I'd gazed over the city waiting for nightfall.

"Thulnara is stunning with the two suns shining over the landscape and the purplish atmosphere. But I need my sunglasses." The light from both suns was too bright for my rupling.

After leaving the built up area, I pointed out the different grasses and the gray one bearing the water droplets. I picked a few and gave them to him to sample.

"Bread. It tastes like bread. Yum. And this one reminds me of pineapple."

When we reached the raging river, I did not trust his new found ability to heat and cool things with his palms. He had a fraction of my ability, and when I told him he would have to study and take exams in order to gain more power, he had refused.

The midwife mused that the baby was sharing their ability with Hanson, and I pictured my two greatest loves hand in hand.

"Are we going to cross?" Hanson jerked his head at the water flowing past us. "You can carry me."

I hesitated. If we went to the other side, the trail led to Idda's village. She had welcomed me and changed the course of my life. But having set me on that path, and revealed herself and our child to Hanson, I was wary of visiting her again. Soothsayers did not welcome people in for a chat. Even princes.

But Hanson gripped my shoulder and pointed to the trees on the far side of the river. He gulped and ran a hand over my back. Even though I was clothed, it calmed him when his palm made contact with the scales and the small spikes. "Can you see that, Kagin? Or am I imagining things?"

I followed his gaze, and there in the midst of the low hanging branches and the trailing vines which had objected to my presence that first evening, I saw me. Not a real me, but a hologram, and beside me stood my rupling smiling. In his arms was a babe, and my arms were wrapped around them both.

"I see us. I see our family." The vision vanished, and Hanson leaned against me as both my hearts raced with joy.

With my hand stroking his hair, he whispered, "All will be well."

"What was that?" I asked as a strange sensation fluttered against me.

My rupling placed my hand on his belly. "Our child is saying hello."

22

HANSON

"WHAT IS THIS FOR AGAIN?" Kagin asked, our second cart full of baby gear. He found my need to rush preparation amusing, but he didn't get it. Half of the items we were purchasing needed to be put together, and that took time, and with me having spent a few days on Thulnara, I was quickly running out of it.

My belly was already to the point I was wearing old joggers of my brother's and a tee shirt that barely fit, which was half the reason we'd driven two hours to get supplies. Any locals seeing me would put two and two together that I was too pregnant too soon. The shifters would get it. Some of them had accelerated births, but humans... heck no.

"That is for the baby to lay in if I need to pee," I snapped. "Sorry. I don't know why I'm so... this." I hated how quick to frustrate I was. "It's called a bouncer and it is basically a safe place for baby to lay down, and it bounces, which babies enjoy." Or human babies enjoy. What if our baby hated all of this? What if he prefered Thulnara. What if...

"Rupling. It is fine. Everything will be fine." He ran his thumb along my mating mark. "We will figure all things out. No decisions will be made for us."

It was as if he could see directly into my worries. "You and I are a team, as you say. And we will decide when it is time."

We'd spoken about where to live and raise our baby. He was next in line to be king, and I would never take that from him. He knew this. It was a conversation we kept coming back to. Kagin would give up everything for me and I for him, which put us in a holding pattern.

The only thing we decided for sure was that I needed to make sure my practice was taken care of, and that while we had a gorgeous nursery being prepared for us on Thulnara, I needed one on Earth.

One filled with everything a baby could ever need based on my shopping patterns.

"I know, my love. It's just... a lot to adjust to very quickly." I leaned into his side.

"This says that it comforts babies and allows them to safely co-sleep. We want that, correct." He reached for yet more baby gear. He was doing it to appease me, and I appreciated it more than words could ever express.

"Thank you." I kissed his cheek. "I think we have everything we could need, and anything else we can order to be delivered. Let's go home and put this all together."

After paying a bazillion and a half dollars, loading the car to the point we could barely fit it all, and driving home, I was good and ready for a nap.

And by good and ready, I meant that I fell asleep waiting for the water to boil for our dinner and didn't wake up for five days.

"Five?" I had to have heard him wrong. "How is that even possible?" And why did Kagin seem not at all fazed by it?

"You are with babe. You need sleep. Next time might be six days."

I flipped the blanket from me and started to climb out of bed. I was ginormous. Like super ginormous.

"I need to pee." I plopped myself on the floor and waddled to the bathroom. I freaking waddled.

I glanced in the mirror on my way out. "Kagin, we have a problem." I placed my hands on my belly, my little one wiggling around inside. Best feeling in the world. Too bad it was shrouded in fear.

"You desire help, my rupling?" He was right there at my side. Of course he was.

"If this is five days, then I will not be able to carry this baby to term. I am already the size of a man about to give birth to twins any day." Or triplets. Had I not been sure of who my babe was and that they would be fine, I'd have sworn there were multiples growing within me. "I still have days left."

"You will be fine, my rupling. Come and see. I fixed all the things. Our baby will have everything you desire." Not an ounce of concern filled his voice. "Come with me, love, and then let me give you food."

He led me to the spare bedroom where, sure enough, every single thing we'd purchased was put together and set up like it belonged in a magazine. "It looks—wow." I tried to wrap my arms around him and failed, my belly in the way.

"I used your computer and found some examples of what the set up was, but we can change it however you want."

"It's... it's perfect." More than. "Thank you."

"Your coloring is off." He brushed my brow with his hand. "You... you are pale... not your normal hue."

I waddled back to the mirror, and sure enough, my face looked awful where it had not only a few minutes earlier. "I think maybe we should go to Thulnara and see the midwife." It wasn't like I could go to a human or even shifter one. "Can we go now?"

"Of course, my love." And we left right then and there.

Even though it was my third trip across the galaxy, it still was surreal, as if maybe I was still sleeping.

Five days. That still didn't seem possible, and yet all evidence said that it was.

I didn't know if Kagin called ahead, however they did that, or if the midwife just sensed it, but they were there greeting us and whisking me away not to a medical room, but to Kagin's quarters.

From the time we entered Thulnara, I held onto Kagin for not only comfort, but so I could understand what was going on around me. This whole waking up and being the size of a small continent was scary enough without having people around me talking in a language I still didn't understand.

"I was surprised I did not see you yesterday," the midwife explained as I gripped Kagin's hand. "I had some concern that maybe you gave birth unassisted and that I failed the crown." They did that thing with their hands clasped together. I needed to ask Kagin more about that, but this was very much not the time. The traveling had me feeling off. Not bad, per se, but not myself either.

"I still have days left." I tried to count and wound up dizzy from it. "I know I do."

"You do not. Your baby is joining us today." They looked at me as if I was a small child who didn't understand basic concepts, but I did, and we still had time.

"How many growth sleeps did they have and for how long?" The midwife looked right past me, and they probably should have. I wasn't doing that well, and staying on my feet was hard enough at this point.

"Just one, and for ten moons."

Ten moons.

"You said I slept for five days!" Had I truly slept for ten? Ten days?

"Yes, five days, ten moons," he repeated.

"Ten moons is ten days on Earth. We have but one, remember." Dawning crossed his eyes, and panic filled me.

Ten days plus a week between not knowing I was pregnant and my time on Thulnara was seventeen days. Add to that the time, and I was at day twenty-two. No wonder I was the size of Nebraska. I was past my due date.

"I am having a baby today?" I didn't feel like I was about to give birth. I just felt... "Owww!" I screamed. And now I did feel like I was about to give birth. "I need to know how to do this. I didn't even take Lamaze."

"Your body knows what to do." The midwife was calm, but of course they were. They weren't the one about to push out an entire person.

"Let's remove your clothing in the bedroom." Kagin broke through my eminent freak out.

I waddled in there and disrobed, my middle starting to tighten up to the point I was crying out again. More hand holding so I could understand the midwife.

"He should stand in position. It is near time."

"Stand?" The midwife did not just say stand. I'd seen plenty of births of all kinds of beings in my lifetime and unless they started on all fours that was not going to happen. And really, even for four-legged creatures, laying down was a thing.

"Humans do not birth in that manner," Kagin explained for me. "I watched many births during his sleep and they almost always are prone."

"Then get him on the bed, because this baby is going to want to meet his First Father soon."

They scurried me to the bed, another contraction roiling through me, this one so unbearable that no sound came from me, my body shaking with pain. "It is time. You are doing well, human." The midwife stepped back to the corner of the room. Where were they going? I needed them. I needed a freaking epidural.

"I am here, my love. And I will deliver our baby. It is our way. The midwife is here to guide us only." He rubbed a soothing line on both my thighs, giving me the comfort I needed. Something about that simple touch somehow made me feel—I don't know—stronger somehow. "I did not know that wasn't your way until the computer. But that is how we get our names. I will be his First Father, for it is I who holds him first."

I had questions. So many questions. Our baby didn't give a hoot about them. My next contraction was my last, our little one entering this world with a cry that officially became the most beautiful sound in the world, or was it galaxy now?

"Here is our son." Kagin slid on the bed beside me, handing our sweet boy to me, and he instantly began to root around for his breakfast.

"He is blue." Just as I knew he would be. "It will be hard for him to blend in on Earth." And maybe that was the deciding factor in all of this.

Kagin placed his hand behind our son's ear, and the blue faded to the pale skin that matched my own. "That is not a worry, although he is by far the most beautiful baby, so let us not pretend he will blend." He kissed my cheek. "You did so well, rupling."

A voice cleared across the room. In all the chaos, I'd forgotten we weren't alone. "Might I examine your rupling and your son, your highness." It was the first time I heard them be so formal, and it set me on edge.

"Is... is something wrong?" I asked Kagin, my voice shaking.

"No, my love. It is just customary to formally ask in times such as this."

"Okay," I agreed, and the midwife came over.

"My fathers are on their way," Kagin announced mid-exam. That wasn't awkward at all or anything.

That had the midwife hurrying up and Kagin covering me up with a blanket just as they arrived.

"We have arrived to meet our first grandchild," Kagin's Second Father, who insisted I call him the same, said, a smile on his face. "Have you decided on a name?"

Both of Kagin's parents welcomed me as their own and it was everything. They loved me because Kagin did. That was a kind of unconditional love that truly was just that—unconditional.

"No." I'd known he was coming since before I met Kagin, and I'd thought about it not at all. Not. Once. "Kagin?"

"A Thulnaran and a human name would be best," my First Father—wow, that felt surreal to even think about—said.

"I was thinking Scotull. The humans have a name Scott and Scotull is a common name here." I looked up to Kagin, so grateful he had the time to do all of this while I basically hibernated.

"You are the best mate a human could ever ask for." I leaned into his side.

"And you, my rupling, are the best mate an izleen could ever have."

"We must be off," the king announced. "It is time to ring the bells throughout the land. Our grandson Scotull is here, and the entirety of Thulnara will celebrate."

They left, the midwife behind them, leaving just the three of us nestled on the bed together.

"I love you, Kagin. Thank you for crossing the galaxy to bring me my family."

"As I love you, Hanson. Thank you for making my hearts whole." He placed his hand behind our son's ear, removing the glamour. "And thank you, Scotull, for making me the First Father I always dreamed I'd one day become."

Our little guy let out his first burp.

"I guess we know where he stands on that," I teased. I kissed his sweet head.

We sat there, just watching our son, basking in our love.

I was a dad.

EPILOGUE

HANSON

"DOES THIS NEED MORE GARLIC?" I asked for the third time. Fair to say I was beyond nervous. It was the first time my mate's family was coming to Earth, and the first time they would see our home here.

We'd been traveling back and forth, and First Father was getting antsy about it. He never blatantly said we needed to pick a place specifically, but it was time.

I refused to make the decision for Kagin. Did I love my job? Absolutely. Would I be happy staying here until he needed to step into his place as King of Thulnara? Without a doubt. Would I stand in his way if he needed us to move there earlier to prepare? Never.

But it would be hard. I couldn't do what I did here, there. I didn't know enough about the different species and ecosystem as a whole. There was no way I could be a doctor for their pets.

But I could be a dad and a good mate to Kagin, supporting him as he took his place as ruler of his kind. And really, if I had my rupling and my child, what more could I want? *My animals.* I had to not think too much about that.

"It is perfect. You are perfect. The house is perfect, and of course—Scott is perfect." Our sweet son was asleep in Kagin's arms.

"Are you sure they can find the place?" It wasn't like they could use their GPS.

"They are almost here." A knock came on the door. "See."

"You heard them?" I hadn't thought he had super hearing, but then again, I was constantly discovering new and wonderful things about him.

"Saw them through the window," he said with a smirk, and I walked around to let them in, only to be greeted by Second Father holding a handful of leaves.

"We read this was customary," he explained as he handed them to me. I was glad to be at the point where most of the time we could chat without me needing the help of my personal translator, Kagin's touch.

I still held onto him as often as I could, though... because ruplings.

"Thank you." I took them graciously and got out of their way so they could come in for the real reason for the visit: to snuggle their grandbaby.

I shut the door behind them, and Herix, my brother-in-law, was already holding Scott and making faces at him. Scott adored his uncle. I got it—he was a big kid himself.

"Maybe it's time to settle down and have one of your own, brother." Kagin chuckled.

"I'll leave that to you and our little heir apparent." He singsonged the last bit.

"About that." Kagin came up behind me. "First Father, I have made a decision. I am forfeiting the crown. My place is here with my rupling. This is where he thrives, and I could not be happy denying him that." He wrapped his arms around me from behind, my jaw hanging open.

We had not talked about this. Not. At. All. His parents were going to hate me.

Only they didn't. Next thing I knew, I was in a four-way hug with them.

"Son, you make us so proud," First Father said. "A good Thulnaran keeps his responsibilities—a great Thulnaran puts his rupling above all."

We hugged and some tears were shed, Herix sitting there with Scott the entire time not saying a word.

"Brother." Kagin stepped over to him. "What is upsetting you?" I hadn't noticed his distress until that point.

"Not distress. It's just... king? Me?"

"You," his entire family said at once.

"I have a lot to learn," he said after a long pause.

"And a mate to find," Kagin teased. "Now let us eat the food my rupling prepared with primitive tools. I assure you, it is delicious."

We ate, talked about the future, laughed, and played with Scott. It was the perfect afternoon with my new family.

"Are you sure?" I asked when they went home.

"The only thing I'm more sure about is my love for you both." He kissed Scott's head and then my cheek. "And this—this is where we belong."

"You are where I belong, my rupling, you are."

NEWSLETTERS

Keep up to date on all Lorelei's new releases by signing up for her email here

If you would like to subscribe to Colbie's newsletter, get updates on new releases and promotions, and receive a 6,000-word short story, Ring In The New Year, please visit her website here

NEXT IN THE SERIES…

Sometimes, when you can't find your mate, it's because you haven't looked far enough.

Omega Prince Helix's life is turned upside down when his brother and future king of Thulnara finds his mate on Earth and gives up his crown to begin his life there. Thrust into the position of heir apparent, Helix needs to not only prepare to take the throne, but also find his true mate. If he fails, one will be chosen for him. After seeking advice from his brother, Helix breaks the laws of his kind and finds Idda, a soothsayer. She sees his mate, but there is a problem: His mate is on Earth. Not that Helix plans to let that stop him.

Alpha Lennox loves running the small bed and breakfast his grandfather left for him. It might be the smallest in town, but it has heart. He adores looking after his guests and meeting new people from around the globe who come to stay in his small seaside tourist town. As high season rolls in, his *No Vacancy* sign becomes a permanent fixture. Only there is a vacancy, one he is saving for someone special, someone he saw in a dream, someone he knows deep down is coming just for him.

And then one day, the guest of his dreams arrives and the only place Lennox wants him to stay is by his side...and in his bed.

The Alien Prince's Alpha is the second book in the Close Encounters of the Mating Kind series by the popular co-writing duo of Lorelei M Hart and Colbie Dunbar. It is a sweet with knotty heat alien romance set in the world of Dates of Our Lives. The Alien Prince's Alpha features an alien prince and suddenly future King of Thulnara who is longing for his true mate, a human who thinks the strangest beings out there are the guests at his B&B, an intergalactic meeting of the in-laws, an extra-long appendage that allows for double the fun, true fated mates, and an adorable baby. If you like your sci-fi light, your royalty smexy, your omegas a bit orange around the edges, and your mpreg with heart, download your copy today.

Order Now

Printed in Great Britain
by Amazon

62761999R00092